P9-AGG-572

# THE SUN
# IS NOT
# MERCIFUL

Also by Anna Lee Walters:

*The Sacred: Ways of Knowledge, Sources of Life* (co-author)

# THE SUN IS NOT MERCIFUL

### Short Stories by
## ANNA LEE WALTERS

Firebrand
Books
Ithaca, New York 14850

Stories from this collection have been published in the following books and periodicals: *Earth Power Coming*, ed. Simon Ortiz (Navajo Community College Press), *Frontiers, A Gathering Of Spirit*, ed. Beth Brant (Sinister Wisdom Books), *The Indian Historian*, and *North Dakota Quarterly*.

*Copyright* © 1985 by Anna Lee Walters
"Mythomania" © The American Indian HIstorical Society, 1977
All rights reserved.
This book may not be reproduced in whole or in part, except in the case of reviews, without permission of Firebrand Books, 141 The Commons, Ithaca, New York 14850.

Book design by Loretta Heimbuch
Cover design by Betsy Bayley and Misti Wilcox
Illustrations by Alice Muhlback based on traditional Pawnee motifs
Typesetting by Tracy Hammer

Printed on acid-free paper in the United States by McNaughton & Gunn

**Library of Congress Cataloging-in-Publication Data**

Walters, Anna Lee, 1946-
  The sun is not merciful.

Contents: The warriors—Mythomania—Going home
    —[etc.]
  1. Indians of North America—Fiction    I. Title.
PS3573.A816S8   1985    813'.54    85-16177
ISBN 0-932379-11-7
ISBN 0-932379-10-9 (pbk.)

To all storytellers and to the children,

especially Crystal Dawn.

# Acknowledgments

There are many people to be thanked for their part in making my stories. I would like to thank two people here for their involvement. Rudy Anaya always expected something better, something more from me and challenged me not to settle for anything less than the best I could do. And Bonnie Begay typed all these stories in her spare time. Rudy Anaya was very tough and firm, and Bonnie was so easy to please; she liked everything she typed. Thank you both.

# Contents

# THE WARRIORS

*I*n our youth, we saw hobos come and go, sliding by our faded white house like wary cats who did not want us too close. Sister and I waved at the strange procession of passing men and women hobos. Just between ourselves, Sister and I talked of that hobo parade. We guessed at and imagined the places and towns we thought the hobos might have come from or had been. Mostly they were White or Black people. But there were Indian hobos, too. It never occurred to Sister and me that this would be Uncle Ralph's end.

Sister and I were little, and Uncle Ralph came to visit us. He lifted us over his head and shook us around him like gourd rattles. He was Momma's younger brother, and he could have disciplined us if he so desired. That was part of our custom. But he never did. Instead, he taught us Pawnee words. "*Pari* Is Pawnee and *pita* is man," he said. Between the words, he tapped out drumbeats with his fingers on the table top, ghost dance and round dance songs that he suddenly remembered and sang. His melodic voice lilted over us and hung around the corners of the house for days. His stories of life and death were fierce and gentle. Warriors dangled in delicate balance.

He told us his version of the story of *Pahukatawa*, a Skidi Pawnee warrior. He was killed by the Sioux, but the animals, feeling compassion for him, brought *Pahukatawa* to life again. "The Evening Star and the Morning Star bore children and some people say that these offspring are who we are," he often said. At times he pointed to those stars and greeted them by their Pawnee names. He liked to pray for Sister and me, for everyone and every tiny thing in the world, but we never heard him ask for anything for himself from *Atius*, the Father.

"For beauty is why we live," Uncle Ralph said when he talked of precious things only the Pawnees know. "We die for it, too." He called himself an ancient Pawnee warrior when he was quite young. He told us that warriors must brave all storms and odds and stand their ground. He knew intimate details of every battle the Pawnees ever fought since Pawnee time began, and Sister and I knew even then that Uncle Ralph had a great battlefield of his own.

As a child I thought that Uncle Ralph had been born into the wrong time. The Pawnees had been ravaged so often by then. The tribe of several thousand when it was at its peak over a century before were then a few hundred people who had been closely confined for more than a hundred years. The warrior life was gone. Uncle Ralph was trapped in a transparent bubble of a new time. The bubble bound him tight as it blew around us.

Uncle Ralph talked obsessively of warriors, painted proud warriors who shrieked poignant battle cries at the top of their lungs and died with honor. Sister and I were little then, lost from him in the world of children who saw everything with children's eyes. And though we saw with wide eyes the painted warriors that he fantasized and heard their fierce and haunting battle cries, we did not hear his. Now that we are old and Uncle Ralph has been gone for a long time, Sister and I know that when he died, he was tired and alone. But he was a warrior.

The hobos were always around in our youth. Sister and I were curious about them, and this curiosity claimed much of our time. They crept by the house at all hours of the day and night, dressed in rags and odd clothing. They wandered to us from the railroad tracks where they had leaped from slow-moving boxcars onto the flatland. They hid in high clumps of weeds and brush that ran along the fence near the tracks. The hobos usually traveled alone, but Sister and I saw them come together, like poor families, to share a can of beans or a tin of sardines that they ate with sticks or twigs. Uncle Ralph also watched them from a distance.

One early morning, Sister and I crossed the tracks on our way to school and collided with a tall, haggard whiteman. He wore a very old-fashioned pin-striped black jacket covered with lint and soot. There was fright in his eyes when they met ours. He scurried around us, quickening his pace. The pole over his shoulder where his possessions hung in a bundle at the end bounced as he nearly ran from us.

"Looks just like a scared jackrabbit," Sister said, watching him dart away.

That evening we told Momma about the scared man. She warned us about the dangers of hobos as our father threw us a stern look. Uncle Ralph was visiting but he didn't say anything. He stayed the night and Sister asked him, "Hey, Uncle Ralph, why do you suppose they's hobos?"

Uncle Ralph was a large man. He took Sister and put her on one knee. "You see, Sister," he said, "hobos are a different kind. They see things in a different way. Them hobos are kind of like us. We're not like other people in some ways and yet we are. It has to do with what you see and feel when you look at this old world."

His answer satisfied Sister for a while. He taught us some more Pawnee words that night.

Not long after Uncle Ralph's explanation, Sister and I surprised a Black man with white whiskers and fuzzy hair. He was climbing through the barbed-wire fence that marked our property line. He wore faded blue overalls with pockets stuffed full of handkerchiefs. He wiped sweat from his face. When it dried, he looked up and saw us. I remembered what Uncle Ralph had said and wondered what the Black man saw when he looked at us standing there.

"We might scare him," Sister said softly to me, remembering the whiteman who had scampered away.

Sister whispered, "Hi," to the Black man. Her voice was barely audible.

"Boy, it's sure hot," he said. His voice was big and he smiled.

"Where are you going?" Sister asked.

"Me? Nowheres, I guess," he muttered.

"Then what you doing here?" Sister went on. She was bold for a seven-year-old kid. I was older but I was also quieter. "This here place is ours," she said.

He looked around and saw our house with its flowering mimosa trees and rich green mowed lawn stretching out before him. Other houses sat around ours.

"I reckon I'm lost," he said.

Sister pointed to the weeds and brush further up the road. "That's where you want to go. That's where they all go, the hobos."

I tried to quiet Sister but she didn't hush. "The hobos stay up there," she said. "You a hobo?"

He ignored her question and asked his own. "Say, what is you all? You not Black, you not White. What is you all?"

Sister looked at me. She put one hand on her chest and the other hand on me. "We Indians!" Sister said.

He stared at us and smiled again. "Is that a fact?" he said.

"Know what kind of Indians we are?" Sister asked him.

He shook his fuzzy head. "Indians is Indians, I guess," he said.

Sister wrinkled her forehead and retorted, "Not us! We not like others. We see things different. We're Pawnees. We're warriors!"

I pushed my elbow into Sister's side. She quieted.

The man was looking down the road and he shuffled his feet. "I'd best go," he said.

Sister pointed to the brush and weeds one more time. "That way," she said.

He climbed back through the fence and brush as Sister yelled, "Bye now!" He waved a damp handkerchief.

Sister and I didn't tell Momma and Dad about the Black man. But much later Sister told Uncle Ralph every word that had been exchanged with the Black man. Uncle Ralph listened and smiled.

Months later when the warm weather had cooled and Uncle Ralph came to stay with us for a couple of weeks, Sister and I went to the hobo place. We had planned it for a long time. That afternoon when we pushed away the weeds, not a hobo was in sight.

The ground was packed down tight in the clearing among the high weeds. We walked around the encircling brush and found folded cardboards stacked together. Burned cans in assorted sizes were stashed under the cardboards, and there were remains of old fires. Rags were tied to the brush, snapping in the hard wind.

Sister said, "Maybe they're all in the boxcars now. It's starting to get cold."

She was right. The November wind had a bite to it

and the cold stung our hands and froze our breaths as we spoke.

"You want to go over to them boxcars?" she asked. We looked at the Railroad Crossing sign where the boxcars stood.

I was prepared to answer when a voice roared from somewhere behind us.

"Now, you young ones, you git on home! Go on! Git!"

A man crawled out of the weeds and looked angrily at us. His eyes were red and his face was unshaven. He wore a red plaid shirt with striped gray and black pants too large for him. His face was swollen and bruised. An old woolen pink scarf hid some of the bruise marks around his neck, and his topcoat was splattered with mud.

Sister looked at him. She stood close to me and told him defiantly, "You can't tell us what to do! You don't know us!"

He didn't answer Sister but tried to stand. He couldn't. Sister ran to him and took his arm and pulled on it. "You need help?" she questioned.

He frowned at her but let us help him. He was tall. He seemed to be embarrassed by our help.

"You Indian, ain't you?" I dared to ask him.

He didn't answer me but looked at his feet as if they could talk so he wouldn't have to. His feet were in big brown overshoes.

"Who's your people?" Sister asked. He looked to be about Uncle Ralph's age when he finally lifted his face and met mine. He didn't respond for a minute. Then he sighed. "I ain't got no people," he told us as he tenderly stroked his swollen jaw.

"Sure you got people. Our folks says a man's always got people," I said softly. The wind blew our clothes and covered the words.

But he heard. He exploded like a firecracker. "Well, I don't! I ain't got no people! I ain't got nobody!".

"What you doing out here anyway?" Sister asked. "You hurt? You want to come over to our house?"

"Naw," he said. "Now you little ones, go on home. Don't be walking round out here. Didn't nobody tell you little girls ain't supposed to be going round by themselves? You might git hurt."

"We just wanted to talk to hobos," Sister said.

"Naw, you don't. Just go on home. Your folks is probably looking for you and worrying bout you."

I took Sister's arm and told her we were going home. Then we said "Bye" to the man. But Sister couldn't resist a few last words, "You Indian, ain't you?"

He nodded his head like it was a painful thing to do. "Yeah, I'm Indian."

"You ought to go on home yourself," Sister said. "Your folks probably looking for you and worrying bout you."

His voice rose again as Sister and I walked away from him. "I told you kids, I don't have no people!" There was exasperation in his voice.

Sister would not be outdone. She turned and yelled, "Oh yeah? You Indian ain't you? Ain't you?" she screamed. "We your people!"

His topcoat and pink scarf flapped in the wind as we turned away from him.

We went home to Momma and Dad and Uncle Ralph then. Uncle Ralph met us at the front door. "Where you all been?" he asked looking toward the railroad tracks. Momma and Dad were talking in the kitchen.

"Just playing, Uncle," Sister and I said simultaneously.

Uncle Ralph grabbed both Sister and I by our hands and yanked us out the door. "*Awkuh!*" he said, using the Pawnee expression to show his dissatisfaction.

Outside, we sat on the cement porch. Uncle Ralph was quiet for a long time, and neither Sister nor I knew what to expect.

"I want to tell you all a story," he finally said. "Once,

there were these two rats who ran around everywhere and got into everything all the time. Everything they were told not to do, well they went right out and did. They'd get into one mess and then another. It seems that they never could learn."

At that point Uncle Ralph cleared his throat. He looked at me and said, "Sister, do you understand this story? Is it too hard for you? You're older."

I nodded my head up and down and said, "I understand."

Then Uncle Ralph looked at Sister. He said to her, "Sister, do I need to go on with this story?"

Sister shook her head from side to side. "Naw, Uncle Ralph," she said.

"So you both know how this story ends?" he said gruffly. Sister and I bobbed our heads up and down again.

We followed at his heels the rest of the day. When he tightened the loose hide on top of his drum, we watched him and held it in place as he laced the wet hide down. He got his drumsticks down from the top shelf of the closet and began to pound the drum slowly.

"Where you going, Uncle Ralph?" I asked. Sister and I knew that when he took his drum out, he was always gone shortly after.

"I have to be a drummer at some doings tomorrow," he said.

"You a good singer, Uncle Ralph," Sister said. "You know all them old songs."

"The young people nowadays, it seems they don't care bout nothing that's old. They just want to go to the Moon." He was drumming low as he spoke.

"We care, Uncle Ralph," Sister said.

"Why?" Uncle Ralph asked in a hard, challenging tone that he seldom used on us.

Sister thought for a moment and then said, "I guess because you care so much, Uncle Ralph."

His eyes softened as he said, "I'll sing you an *Eruska* song, a song for the warriors."

The song he sang was a war dance song. At first Sister and I listened attentively, but then Sister began to dance the man's dance. She had never danced before and tried to imitate what she had seen. Her chubby body whirled and jumped the way she'd seen the men dance. Her head tilted from side to side the way the men moved theirs. I laughed aloud at her clumsy effort, and Uncle Ralph laughed heartily, too.

Uncle Ralph went in and out of our lives after that. We heard that he sang at one place and then another, and people came to Momma to find him. They said that he was only one of a few who knew the old ways and the songs.

When he came to visit us, he always brought something to eat. The Pawnee custom was that the man, the warrior, should bring food, preferably meat. Then, whatever food was brought to the host was prepared and served to the man, the warrior, along with the host's family. Many times Momma and I, or Sister and I, came home to an empty house to find a sack of food on the table. Momma or I cooked it for the next meal, and Uncle Ralph showed up to eat.

As Sister and I grew older, our fascination with the hobos decreased. Other things took our time, and Uncle Ralph did not appear as frequently as he did before.

Once while I was home alone, I picked up Momma's old photo album. Inside was a gray photo of Uncle Ralph in an army uniform. Behind him were tents on a flat terrain. Other photos showed other poses but only in one picture did he smile. All the photos were written over in black ink in Momma's handwriting. *Ralphie in Korea*, the writing said.

Other photos in the album showed our Pawnee relatives. Dad was from another tribe. Momma's momma was in the album, a tiny gray-haired woman who no longer lived. And Momma's momma's dad was in the album; he wore old Pawnee leggings and the long feathers of a dark bird sat upon his head. I closed the album when Momma, Dad, and Sister came home.

Momma went into the kitchen to cook. She called me and Sister to help. As she put on a bibbed apron, she said, "We just came from town, and we saw someone from home there." She meant someone from her tribal community.

"This man told me that Ralphie's been drinking hard," she said sadly. "He used to do that quite a bit a long time ago, but we thought it had stopped. He seemed to be all right for a few years." We cooked and then ate in silence.

Washing the dishes, I asked Momma, "How come Uncle Ralph never did marry?"

Momma looked up at me but was not surprised by my question. She answered, "I don't know, Sister. It would have been better if he had. There was one woman who I thought he really loved. I think he still does. I think it had something to do with Mom. She wanted him to wait."

"Wait for what?" I asked.

"I don't know," Momma said, and sank into a chair.

After that we heard unsettling rumors of Uncle Ralph drinking here and there.

He finally came to the house once when only I happened to be home. He was haggard and tired. His appearance was much like that of the whiteman that Sister and I met on the railroad tracks years before.

I opened the door when he tapped on it. Uncle Ralph looked years older than his age. He brought food in his arms. "*Nowa*, Sister," he said in greeting. "Where's the other one?" He meant my sister.

"She's gone now, Uncle Ralph. School in Kansas," I

answered. "Where you been, Uncle Ralph? We been worrying about you."

He ignored my question and said, "I bring food. The warrior brings home food. To his family, to his people." His face was lined and had not been cleaned for days. He smelled of cheap wine.

I asked again, "Where you been, Uncle Ralph?"

He forced himself to smile. "Pumpkin Flower," he said, using the Pawnee name, "I've been out with my warriors all this time."

He put one arm around me as we went to the kitchen table with the food. "That's what your Pawnee name is. Now don't forget it."

"Did somebody bring you here, Uncle Ralph, or are you on foot?" I asked him.

"I'm on foot," he answered. "Where's your Momma?"

I told him that she and Dad would be back soon. I started to prepare the food he brought.

Then I heard Uncle Ralph say, "Life is sure hard sometimes. Sometimes it seems I just can't go on."

"What's wrong, Uncle Ralph?" I asked.

Uncle Ralph let out a bitter little laugh. "What's wrong?" he repeated. "What's wrong? All my life, I've tried to live what I've been taught, but Pumpkin Flower, some things are all wrong!"

He took a folded pack of Camel cigarettes from his coat pocket. His hand shook as he pulled one from the pack and lit the end. "Too much drink," he said sadly. "That stuff is bad for us."

"What are you trying to do, Uncle Ralph?" I asked him.

"Live," he said.

He puffed on the shaking cigarette a while and said, "The old people said to live beautifully with prayers and song. Some died for beauty, too."

"How do we do that, Uncle Ralph, live for beauty?" I asked.

"It's simple, Pumpkin Flower," he said. "Believe!"

"Believe what?" I asked.

He looked at me hard. "*Awkuh!*" he said. "That's one of the things that is wrong. Everyone questions. Everyone doubts. No one believes in the old ways anymore. They want to believe when it's convenient, when it doesn't cost them anything and they get something in return. There are no more believers. There are no more warriors. They are all gone. Those who are left only want to go to the Moon."

A car drove up outside. It was Momma and Dad. Uncle Ralph heard it too. He slumped in the chair, resigned to whatever Momma would say to him.

Momma came in first. Dad then greeted Uncle Ralph and disappeared into the back of the house. Custom and etiquette required that Dad, who was not a member of Momma's tribe, allow Momma to handle her brother's problems.

She hugged Uncle Ralph. Her eyes filled with tears when she saw how thin he was and how his hands shook.

"Ralphie," she said, "you look awful, but I am glad to see you."

She then spoke to him of everyday things, how the car failed to start and the latest gossip. He was silent, tolerant of the passing of time in this way. His eyes sent me a pleading look while his hands shook and he tried to hold them still.

When supper was ready, Uncle Ralph went to wash himself for the meal. When he returned to the table, he was calm. His hands didn't shake so much.

At first he ate without many words, but in the course of the meal he left the table twice. Each time he came back, he was more talkative than before, answering Momma's questions in Pawnee. He left the table a third time and Dad rose.

Dad said to Momma, "He's drinking again. Can't you tell?" Dad left the table and went outside.

Momma frowned. A determined look grew on her face.

When Uncle Ralph sat down to the table once more, Momma told him, "Ralphie, you're my brother but I want you to leave now. Come back when you're sober."

He held a tarnished spoon in mid-air and put it down slowly. He hadn't finished eating, but he didn't seem to mind leaving. He stood, looked at me with his red eyes, and went to the door. Momma followed him. In a low voice she said, "Ralphie, you've got to stop drinking and wandering—or don't come to see us again."

He pulled himself to his full height then. His frame filled the doorway. He leaned over Momma and yelled, "Who are you? Are you God that you will say what will be or will not be?"

Momma met his angry eyes. She stood firm and did not back down.

His eyes finally dropped from her face to the linoleum floor. A cough came from deep in his throat.

"I'll leave here," he said. "But I'll get all my warriors and come back! I have thousands of warriors and they'll ride with me. We'll get our bows and arrows. Then we'll come back!" He staggered out the door.

In the years that followed, Uncle Ralph saw us only when he was sober. He visited less and less. When he did show up, he did a tapping ritual on our front door. We welcomed the rare visits. Occasionally he stayed at our house for a few days at a time when he was not drinking. He slept on the floor.

He did odd jobs for minimum pay but never complained about the work or money. He'd acquired a vacant look in his eyes. It was the same look that Sister and I had seen in the hobos when we were children. He wore a similar careless array of clothing and carried no property with him at all.

The last time he came to the house, he called me by

my English name and asked if I remembered anything of all that he'd taught me. His hair had turned pure white. He looked older than anyone I knew. I marvelled at his appearance and said, "I remember everything." That night I pointed out his stars for him and told him how *Pahukatawa* lived and died and lived again through another's dreams. I'd grown, and Uncle Ralph could not hold me on his knee anymore. His arm circled my waist while we sat on the grass.

He was moved by my recitation and clutched my hand tightly. He said, "It's more than this. It's more than just repeating words. You know that, don't you?"

I nodded my head. "Yes, I know. The recitation is the easiest part but it's more than this, Uncle Ralph."

He was quiet, but after a few minutes his hand touched my shoulder. He said, "I couldn't make it work. I tried to fit the pieces."

"I know," I said.

"Now before I go," he said, "do you know who you are?"

The question took me by surprise. I thought very hard. I cleared my throat and told him, "I know that I am fourteen. I know that it's too young."

"Do you know that you are a Pawnee?" he asked in a choked whisper.

"Yes Uncle," I said.

"Good," he said with a long sigh that was swallowed by the night.

Then he stood and said, "Well, Sister, I have to go. Have to move on."

"Where are you going?" I asked. "Where all the warriors go?" I teased.

He managed a smile and a soft laugh. "Yeah, wherever the warriors are, I'll find them."

I said to him, "Before you go, I want to ask you... Uncle Ralph, can women be warriors too?"

He laughed again and hugged me merrily. "Don't tell me you want to be one of the warriors too?"

"No, Uncle," I said, "Just one of yours." I hated to let him go because I knew I would not see him again.

He pulled away. His last words were, "Don't forget what I've told you all these years. It's the only chance not to become what everyone else is. Do you understand?"

I nodded and he left.

I never saw him again.

The years passed quickly. I moved away from Momma and Dad and married. Sister left before I did.

Years later in another town, hundreds of miles away, I awoke in a terrible gloom, a sense that something was gone from the world the Pawnees knew. The despair filled days, though the reason for the sense of loss went unexplained. Finally, the telephone rang. Momma was on the line. She said, "Sister came home for a few days not too long ago. While she was here and alone, someone tapped on the door, like Ralphie always does. Sister yelled, 'Is that you, Uncle Ralphie? Come on in.' But no one entered."

Then I understood that Uncle Ralph was dead. Momma probably knew too. She wept softly into the phone.

Later Momma received an official call confirming Uncle Ralph's death. He had died from exposure in a hobo shanty, near the railroad tracks outside a tiny Oklahoma town. He'd been dead for several days and nobody knew but Momma, Sister, and me.

Momma reported to me that the funeral was well attended by the Pawnee people. Uncle Ralph and I had said our farewells years earlier. Momma told me that someone there had spoken well of Uncle Ralph before they put him in the ground. It was said that "Ralphie came from a fine family, an old line of warriors."

Ten years later, Sister and I visited briefly at Momma's and Dad's home. We had been separated by hundreds of miles for all that time. As we sat under Momma's flowering mimosa trees, I made a confession to Sister. I said, "Sometimes I wish that Uncle Ralph were here. I'm a grown woman but I still miss him after all these years."

Sister nodded her head in agreement. I continued. "He knew so many things. He knew why the sun pours its liquid all over us and why it must do just that. He knew why babes and insects crawl. He knew that we must live beautifully or not live at all."

Sister's eyes were thoughtful, but she waited to speak while I went on. "To live beautifully from day to day is a battle all the way. The things that he knew are so beautiful. And to feel and know that kind of beauty is the reason that we should live at all. Uncle Ralph said so. But now, there is no one who knows what that beauty is or any of the other things that he knew."

Sister pushed back smokey gray wisps of her dark hair. "You do," she pronounced. "And I do, too."

"Why do you suppose he left us like that?" I asked.

"It couldn't be helped," Sister said. "There was a battle on."

"I wanted to be one of his warriors," I said with an embarrassed half-smile.

She leaned over and patted my hand. "You are," she said. Then she stood and placed one hand on her bosom and one hand on my arm. "We'll carry on," she said.

I touched her hand resting on my arm. I said, "Sister, tell me again. What is the battle for?"

She looked down toward the fence where a hobo was coming through. We waved at him.

"Beauty," she said to me. "Our battle is for beauty. It's what Uncle Ralph fought for, too. He often said that everyone else just wanted to go to the Moon. But remember, Sister, you and I done been there. Don't forget, after all, we're children of the stars."

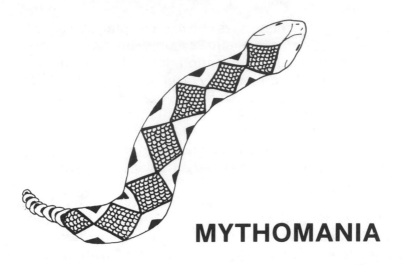

# MYTHOMANIA

*I*n those days and in those places, the sun never rose yellow as told in the myths. There was no sky blue or horizons for that matter, in the distance or in the imagination. If there was a sun, it did not climb the edge of this world. (There was a sun once.) In this place at an appropriate time the world turned light, then dark. Yet even in light, or perhaps because of light, that world, that place, remained dark. There, time was so difficult to judge. And the effort was always more time-consuming than time-saving. Anyway the effort was lost in the myths, as youth was lost in the myths, for the human beings who dwelt in those days and in those places.

Here there was no youth. What was here were human beings, neither male nor female. They were without color and without youth. What was here were human beings that swayed in limbo between living and dying. Always, it was death that swayed closer.

In those days and in those places, when things got old they were thrown away. Accordingly, when human beings grew old, human beings were thrown away.

Therefore in those days and in those places, a sign of age was a bad omen. It meant certain death among other things: confinement, medication, loss of faculties, and loss of beauty (if there was any in those days and in those places). As a result, human beings decided it was better to die young. Always there were the myths.

Beauty? In those days and in those places, the eyes of the beholder were glassy and did not see what they didn't want to see. So they did not ever see beyond the image of themselves.

There was no wisdom in those days and in those places. (There was wisdom once.) There was vanity though, an abundance of vanity. There was youth, yes. But youth was not among the elderly. And youth thrived on the vanity.

Among those vain youths, there were no elders either, as there were no youths among the elderly. For the elderly offended the youths, and the youths banished them and put them in exile. It seems youth feared contamination. So the youths separated themselves. Yet in the meantime both (the elderly and youth) grew older. And youth pretended. The myths were more real.

Consequently there was no dignity among the young because they had never learned it or seen it among their peers. There was no dignity anywhere. (There was dignity once.) The elderly had long since forgotten the necessity of it; the youth didn't want it. The responsibility was too much for either the youths or the aged to carry. So they simply didn't in those days and in those places.

It happened that during those fateful days, but away from these places of exile, a child was being reared on the myths. A child called Firefly, a child of the human beings he was. And yet Firefly was also born of the myths.

Now young Firefly, hearing the wind's rumors of the aged in those days and in those places, resolved to go there. Once there, Firefly planned to run and shoot that enemy down. That is how Firefly planned his kill. Then Firefly challenged his enemy aloud.

"Old Age, I have heard that you are a fool, and an *old* one too!"

And Old Age was silent. If Old Age replied, Firefly did not hear. So this is what happened in those days and in those places. After all, Firefly had been reared on the myths, it is told.

During one dark day, the wind blew Firefly into one of those dark places where the sun did not rise. And Firefly's big round eyes were opened and his mouth, too.

Firefly found himself in a sea of human beings who swam dreamlike before him. His eyes found their sunken eyes. They returned his stare unflinchingly. But they did not actually see Firefly. They had already known too many Fireflies. Also, the myths were full of them.

Until that moment, Firefly never really believed that the elderly existed. Firefly had been taught too well to not see beyond the image of himself. The youths had never mentioned the elderly, except in whispers. And of course, it is now known, the myths are always censored. The ballads of those days and those places did not sing of anything except youth and the myths. But the existence and exile of those human beings was as far from the myths as truth is from the lie.

Firefly was an unbeliever. In those days and in those places, human beings were allowed to believe in only two things, but these two included everything else. First, human beings believed in myths. Then they believed in youth. Everything else was irrelevant.

In exile at those places and during those days were elderly human beings whose skin was golden. Now this was very strange for that place and time because every effort was made to make human beings identical, in appearance and so forth. This was one of the roles of the myths.

On occasion it had been reported that dark-skinned human beings did mysteriously continue to exist. Of course, the myths made no mention of this.

Such was a human being called the Nameless One. As this human being grew older, his skin became more golden. The Nameless One was greatly envied, particularly by youths. This was partly because the Nameless One seemed to become more fit mentally and bodily as he aged. It puzzled and eventually angered the youths.

At his trial it was noted that the golden human being had not visibly aged in the past few years. This was duly recorded. Such things were of importance in those days and in those places.

It happened that the Nameless One was turned in, or turned over, to the proper authorities (coincidentally, who happened to be youths) for practicing "magic." This charge meant impersonating youth. Magic was forbidden in those days and in those places, for the youths said there was little need for it. The youths had something better. They had the myths. In the same breath, they talked of staying young forever and ever.

Youth found the elder guilty of growing old. He was sentenced to imprisonment until death was officially declared. So it was then, and that sentence was being carried out.

He was called the Nameless One because he was a human being without a name. Everything had been stripped from him by plan and deceit, including his names.

As a joke, the youths took his names away. (He had several.) The intent was to take away his breath and identity. The plan failed. In the end, the Nameless One merely acquired another name and a distinguished one at that.

The Nameless One was a human being without bitterness. He did not know that taste of the myths.

Herein was his secret. The youths would have purchased it and paid for it with the myths.

Now that Firefly had made his flight from the myths into exile, he was intent upon finding Old Age before Old Age found Firefly.

The frail human beings who moved hauntingly around him frightened Firefly with their age. Among those human beings were those who were unhearing, unspeaking, and unseeing. Firefly was blissfully unaware that he was more helpless than they.

Far off Firefly heard a human being call out, "Help. H-e-l-p!" Firefly moved in that direction. There he found a pale man shriveled to the bones. His eyes were sunken and glazed. The pale man yelled again, "Help. H-e-l-p!" It echoed around Firefly. In the distance, as in a dream, Firefly heard footsteps, doors unlocking and relocking—safe-keeping for youth and the myths. Then silence.

And Firefly took the cue from the pale man. Firefly yelled, "Help. Help me!"

Over and over Firefly yelled, but none were listening in those days and in those places. Human beings had been screaming in terror of the myths, dying for help since the beginning of those myths. They had yet to be heard.

Finally Firefly made this realization. Firefly sank to his big feet and waited. The wait would be long. Darkness came. (It was always dark in those days and in those places.) Firefly's big eyes wept but not for those elderly human beings. Firefly, being young and reared on the myths, wept for himself. Firefly cried his big eyes to sleep.

It was Firefly's sobbing that the Nameless One heard. The elderly human being came to rescue the young human being. While Firefly slept his myths away, the Nameless One carried Firefly away in his golden arms.

When Firefly woke and flashed his eyes around, he found the Nameless One watching over him. The golden human being spoke, "Child, what brings you here?"

"I came to find Old Age. I came to put Old Age in a grave." All this Firefly said boldly.

The golden human being smiled and said nothing.

Firefly sat at the foot of the Nameless One. They were unspeaking, yet they were in accord. It seemed that they sat only briefly. (There, time was so difficult to judge.) But in truth, they sat for many years pondering upon Old Age. And then the Nameless One made his reply.

"So you hunt Old Age. I do not doubt that you will find Old Age, if you live long enough. Yet, Firefly may as well go in search of the Sun." This was the first advice the Nameless One would ever lend to Firefly. Now there was no Sun in those days and in those places. It had long been replaced with the myths because the myths had more purpose and gave off more fire.

Then a female came forth out of the vague mists of that day and place. She was as old as the wind and as withered as dried roots. She walked with a cane, and it made a mysterious great thump each time it came closer to Firefly. She was unaccustomed to speech. She usually talked with her eyes. They were like stars and outshone the myths.

"Hmmm," says she. "I am called Warrior by the Dark People. I *am* Warrior of the Dark People. It is a name taken from your myths as your name is also. Therefore it is time and place that we should meet. I have known very many fireflies. Always, they look just like you."

With Warrior came her companion who was unseeing. Daydream was blind where his eyes should be. The two had been together since both's beginnings. By the appearance of them, it might have been for eternity. They had crawled on all fours together, took their first stumbling steps together. It had been a long time spent, and they planned how they should leave the world— together.

Warrior and Daydream had a child, who knows how long ago? Shadow was their offspring. Shadow slipped away from Warrior and Daydream on a quest similar to that of Firefly's. Shadow yearned for the secret of eternal youth as did all human beings in those days and in those places. Shadow did not return to Warrior and Daydream. Some people say Shadow found the secret, that Shadow lurks and plays about, always in youth. Others say Shadow became as old and dark as the myths, and that Shadow is still chasing youth around.

Then Daydream spoke, and when he did it sounded like a song. "Firefly seeks Old Age. A conqueror Firefly would be! Well, we shall see."

This conversation which took place appeared to last as long as the eye takes to blink. But in truth, it took many years in those days and in those places.

There, in exile, Firefly remained, for there was no way back. Firefly stubbornly went in search of Old Age asking his way like an infant searching for his mother's breast.

The three accompanied Firefly during this time in that place. Warrior spoke a good deal with her voice and eyes. She was gruff and harsh. Yet of the four, she was the most calm and quiet. She was cruelly honest. Yet she was always fair. She could be ugly, frighten Firefly to tears. Then she could be lovely, beautiful, and steal Firefly's heart away. Her words were often like this. "Firefly! Firefly! My pretty Firefly. Let us climb the walls of this dark time and place together."·

She healed Firefly's lonely body, took up with him his lonely journey. Whenever Firefly hurt, and often he did (from the myths and the pain of them), Warrior pulled feathers out from the sore. And the pain stopped.

Daydream sang Firefly many and many a tune of fools and myths, and how together both fed and grew. Daydream had felt his way through those blind days and had seen many dark places. In song for Firefly, the words and melodies unwound all that Daydream stored or envisioned.

The Nameless One did not speak in words the way Firefly had learned. But the Nameless One was constantly at Firefly's arm, putting thoughts in Firefly's mind and never uttering a word. Often the Nameless One smiled.

In this manner Firefly's vision (and age) grew.

These four probed the myths in those days and in those places with Firefly in search of Old Age. And Firefly did not count the days in the places they visited, nor did they. Time passed, but the dark days, dark places, and the myths remained.

To Firefly, it seemed that he had only arrived. But in those days and in those places, time was so difficult to judge. By then, Firefly had been in search of Old Age for a lifetime.

Therefore, because Firefly stayed in pursuit, Firefly discovered Old Age. Strangely, Firefly was taken by surprise. Firefly found what he had sought for a lifetime. Yet Firefly came to Old Age unprepared.

It happened that the two met face to face in confrontation. Firefly had his companions. Old Age had loyal companions, too.

Firefly had smelled water, thirsted, and found Old Age. In the clear, uncloudy water, Firefly found an image of himself unlike any image he had ever seen. Into the water, he stared. Old Age waited there.

Tears slipped from the corners of Firefly's eyes. Silence. The tears mingled with the water. The image in the water also wept silently in recognition of the other.

"*Aho!* So we meet," whispered Firefly.

And the image whispered, "*Aho!* So we meet."

Firefly sat and examined the picture. The image did likewise. It seemed that they sat for days, but Firefly was lost in time. In truth, they sat much longer.

Now Firefly meditated upon his quest: to strike down and put Old Age in the ground. This, too, is what the image reflected upon (for he was no old fool): to strike down and put Firefly in the ground.

Then Warrior flew to Firefly's side, peeked into the water, and saw why Firefly cried. Said Warrior softly to the image, "Ah." Warrior's word fell like rain on the ground.

With that one word Warrior had bid Daydream to come near. Daydream came forward, felt the word and image that fell. Daydream swirled those telltale waters all around. Touching Firefly's face gently all the while, he understood Firefly's tears. Then Daydream sang a melancholy sound, "Don't cry. You came to conquer! Don't cry."

The Nameless One said nothing all the while, just stood with his head slightly bowed. Nor did the Nameless One smile.

"You knew!" Firefly said accusingly to his companions. "You knew it all the time."

In anger Firefly was bitter. Firefly had come to shoot Old Age down. Now he found that Old Age was a warrior whose deadly aim was straight and true.

Said Warrior calmly to Firefly, "When at first we met, I told you. I am called Warrior by the Dark People. I am Warrior. It is a name taken from your myths as Firefly is also, but warriors and fireflies are as old as the beginning. Therefore it was time and place that we should meet. I have known very many fireflies. Always they act just like you."

"The Dark People were the first people. I am called Warrior which means exactly that. The first warrior was and is Old Age. This is what you see standing before you."

"Firefly, we are all Old Age. Old Age is more than that. You have come in search of us to rid us from youth and myths. Now you are not pleased with what you find."

"Firefly has come from the myths and cannot tell what is real and what is not. Is Firefly real? Old Age is not myth and does not tell lies. Look at Old Age and see the Sun! Old Age is not all misery or unkind!"

Firefly paused briefly and listened. But Firefly did not have a change of heart; and time, unlike before, passed quickly.

Firefly passed from that day and place in bitterness and old age.

The youths did not learn of Firefly's death. Nor was it ever recorded in the myths. Indeed, it is likely that the youths never knew that Firefly ever lived.

The Nameless One passed on in the quiet of later years. The youths did speak of the Nameless One, in jest. In time there were stories that told only of a fool without name. It (the fool) might have been anyone. There were many in those days and in those places. No one recalled the Nameless One. No one recalled that he had other names, the first of which was Firefly.

But Warrior and Daydream often spoke of the Nameless One long after his passing. They had met many human beings and known all the fools, all the myths. It was always the myths that die hard.

The youths continued to live as they always had, apart from the elderly. The myths survived, too.

The elderly of those days and places were never rescued. None (of the human beings) escaped those dark places and dark days except for those who passed away in youth. Ironically, it often was the myths that brought these youths doom. Yet, the youths took pains to preserve the myths which gave youth purpose and fire.

They had no dignity. They had no wisdom. They had no
Sun to light their world. It fell when a mythical youth shot
it down. And none (of the elderly or youth) lived to tell
what happened in those dark places and days.

Warrior and Daydream stayed on looking after the
elderly, for who else would do it? Often fireflies would
pass their way and flutter in the wind.

Then Daydream would sing, "Ah, Firefly! Pretty
Fireflies! Always they flutter their wings in the wind. Ah,
Firefly! Pretty Fireflies! Over the flame they flutter and
drop from the wind!"

# GOING HOME

*H*is name was Sun. The old women and their old men reared him. Under their care he grew into a huge bearlike man they called Sun.

Sun had no woman until he met Nita. It was with her that all this began. She came into his life like a storm blown from the flat prairie land in the east. He found her in the desert, a flower which he picked for himself and carried home.

She was not of his people and was very different from anyone he'd ever known. Nita's people were a few small families who were the sole survivors of a nearly extinct tribe. They made their home hundreds of prairie miles from the desert where Sun lived. A few of Sun's people objected to the "outsider woman" of his. It was a flaw. But he and Nita lived together despite the few objections, and twenty years went quickly. Nita and Sun spent most of that time alone with each other. Nita did carry two children, each for nine months, but Sun buried them beside the house soon after each was born. Their house was quiet during this time.

As Sun looked at Nita one afternoon, he suddenly realized that she had grown old. The afternoon haunted him. He stared at his own rugged face in a cracked mirror for long terrifying hours. He no longer recognized it. Where had the years gone? They'd left him with nothing he could put his finger on but the jagged lines in his face and hands, and a mass of silver hair.

He was a desperate man. He knew it later. Desperation. Later he told himself he should have recognized the desperation earlier. He was older, not wiser. Sun told himself that Nita's beauty had faded and scowled that "Nita has grown too old for me." He grasped at the old flaw—Nita was an outsider woman—who grew old too soon. It was then that he began to look past Nita to other flowers coming into bloom.

Nita became more quiet. She was ever observant and saw more than she wished to see. Before her eyes, Sun became a changed man. His eyes seldom met hers anymore but stayed on the women in abundance around him. The hours Sun was away from their house exceeded the few that he spent with her.

Then Nita began to long for home. The longing became strong. The flat, curving prairie land and the scent of wet, green grass beckoned to her. The handful of people destined for extinction stayed in her thoughts. She was one of them.

When Sun was home, there were few words between them. They were courteous to one another, nothing more. Sun hated to look at Nita and be reminded of the chipping away of time. Her once smooth face was layered with soft tiny creases that looked deeper in daylight. Nita turned away from him whenever she saw frownlines cover his forehead. At rare times Sun's scowl softened, and he thought of reaching for Nita and smoothing her face in his rough hands. He thought of holding her for a little while. But he would not permit himself to touch her anymore.

It was with a twinge of pain and guilt whenever Sun went out alone. When he touched the other woman, he felt the same twinge, the same stab of feeling. He thought to himself then that if Nita were not around, time might slow itself, things would get better. Nita waited for Sun to come home every day, though he was sullen and angry with her most of the time.

While Nita was alone one day, a slender, bold, and youthful woman visited. Nita let her enter the house.

"We desire to marry," she said of herself and Sun to Nita.

He came from work in the late afternoon to find Nita standing at the screen door. Her face was a calm mask, but her eyes burned.

She said through the screen, "If you come in, we'll have to talk. Make up your mind." It was the most she had said in weeks.

The tone of her voice took him by surprise and puzzled him. Slowly he opened the screen door and ducked inside. He asked, "What's wrong?"

Nita pointed at the young woman rising hesitantly to greet him. It took him a few moments to comprehend everything, but when he finally did, he yelled violently at the young woman. She ran from the house with tears sliding down her face.

The house grew mute, deathly solemn. Nita sat in a wooden rocking chair for more than an hour and watched the red sun fall through the window. The rocking chair squeaked with each movement. Sun lay on the bed in another room, staring at the ceiling and listening to the monotonous squeaks of Nita's chair.

Finally, Sun went to Nita and spoke to her. "Nita, I didn't promise her anything," he said.

Nita's eyes did not leave the window. She replied in a voice that resembled a child's. "I've been away from home for so long. I'm sure there's honeysuckle on the vines. The weather will be stifling, but the people are few. It's been too long away from them. Soon they will all be gone. There'll be none of us left anymore." She let out a long sigh. The rocking chair creaked under Nita's voice. Sun was amazed at how young her voice sounded.

"Nita," Sun said, "I didn't mean to hurt you...." His voice was deep and resonant, but he didn't know how to say all the things that needed to be said.

"Things change, Sun," Nita said. "Nothing stays the same, except the mountains. They don't change."

Sun's eye's grew stormy. "Go on home if you want to go," he shouted. "The old folks were right. You don't belong here anyway. You never did!" He paced around her rocking chair. It continued to creak, undisturbed by Sun's anger.

Nita watched him silently, recalling to herself that in their early years he seldom shouted at her. She bit her lip and watched him pace. His next act was predictable. He had acted it out several times before.

He stomped into the kitchen. She knew that he stopped at the cabinet where she stored her dishes and tableware. She heard the cabinet drawer open, as she had several times before. She knew that he searched for the small handgun they kept there. As he rummaged through the cabinet looking for shells for the gun, Sun's angry voice shouted, "If you expect me to ask you to stay, you're going to have a long wait!"

Nita turned to see him put the gun in his pocket. He walked to where Nita sat.

"I don't need you," he said in a low voice, a smile on his face. The tone of his voice was entirely within his control. He said evenly, "I'd shoot myself first before I'd ask you to stay."

Nita's eyes lifted to his. She said, "Take care, Sun. The old folks say that words have a fateful grip on our acts."

Sun felt like hitting her but moved away from her toward the door. At the screen he paused, sure that she would not allow him to leave like this. She never had before. Nita's rocking continued. Then her voice followed, "Sun, when you come back again, I'll not be here anymore," she said.

Sun left. Nita sat a few minutes longer thinking of home. She decided to go. She figured the hours it would take to drive the route east. Then she filled two cardboard boxes with a few possessions and went out the screen door, not bothering to lock the house.

Before long she was driving past the houses belonging to Sun's people. In front of a wooden frame house, an old woman stood hitchhiking. Nita stopped for the elder who peeked in the car window. Seeing Nita, she scrambled inside.

The elder laughed. "I can't move like I once did. And how is Sun?"

Nita did not reply to the question. She asked the elder, "Where do you want to go?"

Her passenger pointed up the road before she turned directly to Nita and asked, "Where are you going, anyway?"

Nita could not ignore the question. She answered, "Home. I'm going home, east. To my people, I mean."

The elder clicked her tongue and nodded. She seemed to understand. She didn't reply for a few moments. She gazed out the window.

"I was thinking that your home is here," she then told Nita. The old lady's eyes were thoughtful as she watched Nita's profile. "How long's it been now? How long you been here?"

"Twenty years," Nita answered.

"Then I would say to you, your home is here," the old lady said.

"I've been away so long. It's time to go home again. See how the people are. There's not too many of us anymore," Nita argued politely.

"Ah. Then go home and see them, your people. Take your time. This place will always be here." As the passenger spoke, she waved her hand to indicate the community beyond. The elder narrowed her eyes and tried her question again. "But how is Sun?"

Nita turned her face away, not wanting to respond.

The elder woman stretched out a hand and put it on Nita's thin shoulder. "There is a lot of talk about Sun these days. I don't know what is true, or if it matters that things be so or not so. Sun is a man. True, he is a bear of a man, but nothing more or less than a man. Now go on home, whichever way it is. Home does have a way of calling its own." She squeezed Nita's shoulder to make her point. Nita stopped soon after and let her passenger off. As she slammed the car door, the elder pointed a bony finger up at the sky and raised her voice to Nita, above the hum of the car engine. "It smells of coming rain. The storm will probably last all night. But in the morning when the sun rises, it will be a sight to behold. It always is."

Nita waved at the elder and drove on the only road out of the village. She noticed Sun's truck parked under the *Tavern* sign.

Over a hundred miles later, Nita stopped in Albuquerque to have her compact car serviced before continuing. She planned to drive the entire night. She left the car at a service station and walked to a nearby restaurant.

The elder's conversation returned to Nita. Nita agreed that Sun was a bear of a man, but a man nonetheless, with all the faults and weaknesses of men. She and Sun had made children together. They were delicate and loved creations. Nita recalled that Sun had said the children would be a gift to her nearly extinct people. But the children didn't live, and her people were almost gone. She was beyond child-rearing years, and Sun's attention had gone to other women.

As she ate her late meal, Nita pondered the endless questions that refused to stop running through her head. Even before the slender young woman came to call, Nita had known about her and Sun. But this young woman had dared to confront Nita with Sun's infidelity. Nita had never experienced that before; she just pretended she didn't know.

Nita sat in the restaurant for over an hour watching the headlights of the moving cars streak past. Then Nita decided to go home.

He was drunk, driving aimlessly about the community. He had left the tavern before eleven, after the bartender refused to serve him anymore. He staggered to his car and weaved it out of town. Several times he found himself in the wrong lane. His eyes wanted to close in sleep. Then he decided to go home, even if it was to an empty house.

He tried to find a turnoff to turn around. He saw the glaring headlights of an approaching car through the fine, soft rain that had started to fall. He barely saw the road. He did not know he was on the wrong side again. Above him the sky thundered far away and lightening briefly lit the clouds, but Sun did not hear the thunder or see the lighted sky.

When the vehicles collided, it was at a high speed. Sun's truck had been moving slower, but the truck was big and heavy. The compact car swerved to the right in an attempt to escape the oncoming blow. Sun hit the car firmly on the driver's side. The little car sailed over the edge of the embankment and tumbled down into darkness.

The truck's motor still ran. Sun stopped and got out of the truck. The stinging drizzle on his face sobered him a little. He pulled a flashlight from under his cab seat and walked around his truck to the edge of the road where the car disappeared. Nothing was there that he could see. The rain pounded down on him and thunder rolled toward him.

He climbed back into his truck and drove off. A few miles down the road he found a turnoff which he took. When the tires of the truck became mired in mud, he rested his head on the steering wheel and fell asleep. His foot pressed down on the brake. It gave off a red warning glow until his heavy foot dropped with a thud to the floor of the cab.

He had a headache when he awakened, and a dry mouth. He had dreamed of an accident. The dream tugged at him; it was so real. The world around him was a dense mass of dark blue. His truck rested in a pool of mud and water. His clothes were damp in places and he was cold. The flashlight was on his lap. The nagging dream lingered in his mind. With it, apprehension was born. He turned on the truck lights. The yellow fingers of light probed the predawn darkness. He turned the key in the ignition and backed the truck out of the mud onto the road again.

His eyes watched and searched, but for what he did not really know. Dawn glowed in the east. The sky was lighting. The landscape with towering pine trees was barely discernible against the sky. Something lay on the road ahead. Sun stopped the truck. It was a coyote ripped apart. He couldn't remember if the dissected animal had been there yesterday or last night. He tried to make meaning of the torn coyote in the fuzzy morning. Sun's eyes lifted with dread from the creature to the road ahead. The ominous feeling in him grew. The edges of the world were then visible in all directions.

Sun did not want to get back in the truck and go further down the road, but he did. Fear gripped him. He clutched the steering wheel tightly. The older people had told him that coyotes were omens.

Absorbed in his confusing thoughts, a glint of metal on the incline of the road ahead startled him. His heart began to pound. He stepped out of the truck. Ahead and behind him, the road was still and quiet. The sky was white, drained of color. A lone pale star sparkled far above him.

He moved toward the compact car that was partially hidden from view. He saw black skid marks and stopped momentarily beside them. He seemed to have no say in what his body did. It acted of its own volition. His legs took him down the incline where the little car lay. The wrecked automobile was vaguely familiar to him. The car lay upside-down. The front of the car pointed up toward the road. His heart raced.

He recognized the car immediately. It was Nita's car. His hands reached inside to her, through broken glass. He knew it was her, but a part of him denied it. He didn't want it to be her. He touched her hand and gently stroked it. He thought of moving her out of the car, but she was pinned. He brushed her hair with his fingers and touched her face, then he released her and climbed up the incline. Once there, his legs buckled under him, and he steadied himself by hanging onto his truck.

The sound of an oncoming car brought him to his senses. He waved his arms wildly at the passing motorist. The car stopped and Sun ran to it. His voice came out in a whisper. "Down there. An accident." He didn't tell the stranger what had happened, and he didn't say that Nita was down there. The figure in the car nodded and drove away.

Sun waited there for someone to come for Nita. He told himself that he would say to them that he found her blooming in the desert sand like a flower and carried her home twenty years earlier. Then he wept. He knew his words were not enough to explain anything. Acts of life and death required more. The words that came to the tip of his tongue were wrong. None could soothe him or change anything.

And because there were no words to comfort him, or to make sense of the bright morning light on this dark day, he did the only thing he could do. He sang. His song was unintelligible, a cry of deep hurt and suffering.

Life went on around him. Flocks of birds fluttered to perch on the barbed-wire fence that ran along both sides of the highway. The chirping birds and Sun's voice floated over a bed of soft purple flowers opening to the day. Sun's song filled the void between him and the world around him.

His song ended. His throat was raspy. His hysteria had subsided. His eyes were clear and cold. He opened the truck door and unlocked the glove compartment. The gun was there. What had Nita said about his words having a grip on his acts? He wrapped the gun in his bearlike hand.

# THE RESURRECTION OF JOHN STINK

*A*ll his life John Stink was a loner. No one knew what his name really was before it became John Stink, and local tribal history says that the name was given to at least one other man in the area. Effie later said that the first man to use the name was earlier called John Looks Pretty or John Pretty Man. It all depended on how it was translated, and by whom. Toward the end of his life there seemed to be some confusion about his tribal status and his relationship with the people to whom he belonged. None of the tribes wanted to claim him at that point. But John Stink spoke the languages of that region. He belonged to one of the tribes that were definitely related.

The tribes had been removed to Indian Territory in the latter part of the nineteenth century. By the turn of the century most of the people had undergone a transformation that encompassed virtually every aspect of their lives, from the intangible spiritual side to their mirroring the appearance of their white neighbors as best they could.

John Stink was the exception. He was always different. These differences, however, weren't always within his control. After all, he was a sick man. As a child he must have been frail because as a man he was never well, or "not right," as the people whispered.

He was a short, thick man, not plump or heavy. He did not look sickly. It was a contradiction the people took very seriously. His legs were bowed, and he covered his feet in plain moccasins decorated on the fold with floral patterns, beaded in an assortment of colors. He also wore a dark vest with beaded green leaves, a curling vine, and red and blue berries winding in a border around his waist and neck. These two adaptations in his apparel were the only differences in his whiteman's clothes that he made and insisted upon. When the moccasins and vest became worn, he quickly replaced them with identical ones. On special occasions he added wide beaded armbands just above the elbows of his long, puffed shirt sleeves. He also had a large black hat that pushed the top of his ears down. Around the hat was tacked a colorful beaded hatband. His long, thin braids that stopped short of his waist annoyed some of his tribesmen. They had closely cropped hair just like the whitemen.

By any standard other than the tribes', John Stink would have been considered a wealthy man. He owned a few acres of land. It wasn't much, but it was enough for John Stink. He had built himself a house on that land, putting it together plank by plank with his own hands. He lived there all his life. The floor was dirt, but later John Stink told Effie that it didn't matter.

He had no family. His old parents died when he reached middle age. He did not father children because no woman would have him, and he did not marry. He did not have any living kin that he or anyone else knew of, and therefore he was considered a poor man.

Besides the fact that he was a poor man, John Stink's other affliction was a mysterious sickness that plagued him since childhood. He had seizures that none of his people had ever seen in any other of their tribesmen. His first attack came upon him when he was no more than eight. It came with a viciousness and ugliness that left John stunned. His playmates drew back from him in horror. It did not stop there but continued for the rest of his life. After that John Stink was always a loner.

Effie first saw John Stink in the church house. He entered late and left early, before the preacher finished the sermon. The few people sitting in the stiff wooden pews stirred uneasily when he came in and sat down. Effie didn't hear him enter at all. But when everyone shuffled around in the benches and looked to the back of the church, she did too. There sat John Stink, alone. He ignored the other disapproving faces and looked at Effie. She smiled. John Stink smiled too. Throughout the service, she watched John Stink and thought she even heard him attempt to sing the hymns in a timid voice that barely climbed above the chorus of the others.

Effie saw John Stink off and on after that for the next few years, but she never had reason to say anything to him. When she was nineteen, an aunt came to her and asked her if she would help out a pitiful old man by cooking and cleaning for him. Effie agreed to it. She soon learned that the man was John Stink.

She walked out to the edge of town where his homestead lay and was greeted by a pack of yelping dogs, ranging from fat pups to decrepit old animals. She knocked on the door. He feebly called to her to come inside. Effie went in to find him in bed in the darkened house, though it was late afternoon. She went over and told him who she was, Effie Grayeyes, and that she had come to cook and clean for him. He looked at her for a while. As he did, Effie wondered if he really was crazy.

Finally he nodded his head affirmatively. She could stay.

She cleaned his little dirt-floor house. Then she made him soup for his supper and brewed some sage tea from leaves she had picked outside. She opened the two windows, one set in each end of the house. The air and light filled the two little rooms. After she carried him his supper, she found that he would not sit, so she propped him up with some quilts. Bringing a basin of water, she splashed his face and hands and dried him off with a piece of calico cloth. He did not protest at all but merely watched her. His eyes followed her movement around him. She touched his braids. Again he did not resist, so she unravelled first one braid and then the other. She combed the coarse white strands into two tight, neat braids. Then she held the soup bowl and let him drink the soup noisily. All the time his eyes were studying her.

After she fed him, she stood him on his shaky legs and walked him to a chair outside the house. Laying some blankets on his legs, she left him sitting there while she changed his bedding and put the old quilts out on the tree limbs to flap in the evening breeze. Then she pulled some water up from the well not far from where he sat and filled a container with the liquid. This she placed beside his bed.

She would have helped him back inside, but this time he did protest, saying that he desired to sit there for a while. Effie had nothing else to do there, so she left when he assured her that he would be all right until she returned the next day. Down the road she turned around to see him sitting there, all alone again. She thought about going back. But as she was deciding what to do, the dogs rounded the corner of the house. Seeing John Stink sitting outside, their tails began to wag while they jumped on him affectionately. She felt better about leaving him then.

The next day when she returned, John Stink was

sitting outside, whittling and humming to himself. She nodded to him and went to her chores.

Their relationship continued for several months, and then into years. She worked for John Stink, cleaning and cooking for him, and several times she nursed him back to health. He paid her with paper money, his income for leasing out a part of his land. He paid her well.

Effie fell in love with John Stink, the way she fell in love with the start of every autumn. Both things touched her soul deeply. She didn't know why she loved him as she did. They hardly spoke. They simply were there together.

She took to staying longer at his house, just to keep an eye on him, in case he needed anything. He was old and moved so slowly. Her fingers sewed quilts as she sat on the single chair outside the house. He sat cross-legged on the ground with his back resting against the house, whittling the afternoon away. Her eyes darted back and forth from him to the quilts in her lap. Or she beaded elaborate flowers on cloth that she could tack onto moccasins or vests at some future time. When he was through whittling and tried to stand, Effie always managed to be nearby to take his hand and let him lift himself up.

In those years, John Stink had many seizures. At first she was afraid of him and found this hard to admit to herself. Once while they were outside together, John Stink called out, "Effie! Effie Grayeyes!"

She got to him just as he landed with a muffled thud on the ground. His face was contorted and one side of his body momentarily convulsed. The seizure passed in a few seconds. He opened his eyes, fully recovered, but there was a deep gash under one of his eyes where he had fallen and landed on a cutting rock. Effie managed to deal with each attack, but each one caused her to grow more frightened for the old man.

One time they went into town together in a wagon

borrowed from her aunt. Effie drove the slow team of horses, and John Stink sang an amusing old song that Effie was surprised he knew. He often surprised her by telling old stories and singing old songs. When they got to town and climbed the steps to the porch of the hardware store, John Stink suddenly looked bewildered and clung fiercely to Effie's arm. She knew by now what it was. Again he said, "Effie!" in a most pleading voice, and he fell. Effie couldn't hold him. He toppled off the porch and split open the back of his head. This time he did not recover as quickly as he always had before. Effie called for help. A crowd gathered on the porch. But none would go near John Stink. Effie begged the crowd to help her put him in the wagon. They looked curiously at her but did not move. John Stink lay unconscious for several minutes. Then his eyes opened. The crowd was still gathered, but when they saw his eyes open and watched him try to get up, they scattered. Effie helped him and dusted him off.

The incident in town worried Effie, so she asked John Stink if she might stay at his little house with him. He didn't say no, and he didn't say yes. He didn't say anything to her but whittled and talked to his many dogs.

By then he had accumulated nearly twenty dogs. Whenever a strange dog approached the house, he brought it in and showed it to Effie, and then he fed it. He loved the dogs dearly, and he told Effie a story about why he loved the animals as he did and why it was that they were attached to men as they were.

John Stink said that a long time ago animals could talk. They gathered together to discuss man who had lately been making a nuisance of himself. Man often got into things without thinking about what he was doing. According to the animals, man was not very smart. Nor did he have any other favorable attributes. In bad weather he was likely to freeze. He had a peculiar odor.

He was not particularly pleasant to look at, and he was much worse to be around. The animals agreed that someone should volunteer to be a companion to man, to keep him out of mischief, and to keep him out of the way of the other animals who could not tolerate him. But the animals couldn't decide who among them should go with man. Each one rose and told the others at the gathering why he did not have compassion for man and consequently could not go with him. The meeting was endless because no one wanted to help man. Finally one animal stood and said that he would go with man and watch him and be his companion. This was the horse. When the horse agreed to this, the dog also had to accept this responsibility because the dog was related to the horse. For this reason, dogs were placed at the side of man, John Stink told Effie.

Effie smiled at his story. She knew how he felt about his dogs. So when she talked to him, asking him to let her stay there with him, she was not at all surprised that he talked to his dogs instead of her.

The next day her aunt drove her back to John Stink's house in the wagon. Effie's blankets and other property were tied in several bundles in the back. Effie climbed down from the wagon and looked up at her aunt.

"I don't know, Effie. This man is not right. If you want me to come and get you, let me know," the aunt said.

Effie frowned up at her and then saw John Stink walking toward her. She handed him a bundle of blankets, took a bundle herself, and threw the others on the ground.

"Good-bye, auntie." She waved the wagon away and never moved from John Stink's house after that.

His seizures were harder then, coming with a fierceness that took Effie's breath away. They also came more often. But between the attacks, she enjoyed living there with John Stink and his dogs.

John Stink received some income from his whittling and from other crafts which the local stores purchased from him and resold. Miniature tipis painted with bright stars and moons were a favorite item in the stores. Fashioning one of these, he sang as he worked on his creation. He told Effie that this time he might put horses and dogs on the tipis he was making, instead of the usual stars and moons. Effie agreed that it was a good idea.

She watched him while he worked, and a wave of affection for him swept over her. He had shrunk in size in the last year, but she knew he was strong. She had decided long ago that he must always have been very strong to endure all the attacks he had in his lifetime.

She noticed the tipi drop from his hands, and she saw him fall after it. He didn't call her name like he often did. He just tumbled to his side. Alarmed, she ran to him and clutched his hand, waiting for his eyes to open. Minutes passed. She went inside and dampened a cloth and brought it out to him. Laying it over his forehead, she called to him, "Old Man. Old Man. Wake up!"

He did not move. The dogs came up and sat around him making peculiar cries and sniffing at him.

Effie did not know what to do. There was no place she could go for help. No one would come, not for John Stink. The white doctor in town might come, she thought, if she had enough money and would go get him. She didn't want to leave John Stink alone.

She made a pallet out of quilts and rolled John Stink onto it. The she sat down beside him and held his short, wide hand. Her long skirts were caked with dirt, but she ignored this. John Stink lay frozen, his chest barely rising and falling. Over an hour passed, and he did not stir. She began to talk. "Wake up, Old Man. Don't leave me here like this. Wake up, Old Man."

She said it over and over until her voice was hoarse.

The sun had moved halfway across the sky. The dogs still lay around John Stink and whimpered.

While Effie was wondering what she would do if John Stink did not wake up this time, two of the dogs stood and walked over to her and then to John Stink. They went right up to his face and began to lick it.

Effie heard John Stink chuckle. A wave of relief spread over her. She still held his hand, then felt him pull it away. She did not hug him, though she wanted to. Instead she said very softly, "Old Man, you really scared me this time."

He smiled at her and touched her braids. Then he went back to work on his tipis until nightfall.

That night as she lay on one side of the house and he on the other, his voice came through the darkness. "Do not fear it. It comes for everyone."

She was not sleeping. She had been thinking that she was no help to him. There was nothing she could do.

"What? Do not fear what, Old Man?" Her own voice traveled the same span of darkness.

"You know," he said. "Do not fear death."

"I don't fear it for myself," she replied. "I fear it for you."

"How is that?" His voice seemed to be perplexed.

"Old Man, I love you," she said. "I love you like I love the wind."

He did not answer for a long time. Then he said, "There is no death, only a change of worlds."

Effie did not reply to that. When he realized that she wouldn't, he told her, "Did I ever tell you about the change of worlds? The story...."

"No, Old Man. Are you just making it up?" she asked in the dark.

He laughed and told her that he would tell her sometime.

They didn't talk any more. He was soon snoring softly, and Effie finally went into a fitful sleep.

John Stink was well for nearly a month. Then another attack came. He did not wake up. Effie knew he wouldn't when he lay unconscious for more than a day. His pulse slowed. His breathing stopped. She covered him with one of the quilts she had sewn and walked into town. When she came back, she brought the white doctor and rode in his wagon. They drove up to John Stink's little house, and all the dogs growled at the unfamiliar man with Effie. She led him into the house. John Stink lay just as she left him. The white doctor examined John Stink for a long time while Effie sat outside stroking the dogs that lay at her feet. He finally came out and said, "Miss Grayeyes, there ain't nothing I can do. I'm sorry."

Effie did not even look at him. She knew what he was going to say.

After he climbed upon his wagon seat, he asked Effie if there was anything else he could do. She shook her head and told him no.

He started to drive off, but before he did he said, "So that is who they've been afraid of all this time. I'd never met him, but I'd heard about him. I wonder how they will feel now that he is dead."

He switched his horses and drove away.

No one came to John Stink's funeral the next day. Only Effie was there with the white doctor. And the dogs.

Effie had asked the doctor for help after all. He persuaded three tribal men to hollow out a shallow ditch in the earth. Over this they constructed a rectangular box of wood that was nearly three feet high. John Stink's final resting place would be like the others in the tribal burial grounds. There, the remains of other burials looked like wooden houses, the length of an outstretched man. The boards of the wooden structures were originally covered over and filled in with earth; then the earth became packed down with the heavy rains. After a time the wind and rains would wash the dirt away, and the boards were left exposed and naked.

The day of the funeral the doctor came around in his wagon. Effie had washed and dressed John Stink and combed his white hair. He wore his most elaborate moccasins and vest, and over his long-sleeved white shirt, she had tied the armbands. Then she draped a black wool blanket, trimmed in wide red and green ribbons, around his neck. She stayed up most of the night, sewing the ribbons on the blanket by the dim lamplight.

They carried John Stink wrapped in one of Effie's handmade quilts to the wagon bed and laid him down. The dogs barked loudly as they put him in. Then they drove to the edge of his land where the men had put up the wooden structure, his burial site. The dogs grew quiet as the wagon left them. The doctor helped Effie put John Stink in the wooden resting place. It was boarded over and nailed down by the doctor. Effie worked with him to heap shovels of dirt on it. Loose earth sifted through the boards and left wide gaps in the mound.

She noticed the dogs. They had followed the wagon. They came over and sniffed around the grave, whimpering as they did before when John Stink did not wake up. Effie talked to them as they settled down around John Stink's burial site. Effie watched them curiously.

She declined a ride back to the house with the doctor and paid him for his help with a wide, beaded belt, something that was intended for John Stink.

Standing alone beside the grave she said, "Old Man, you never did tell me about the change of worlds." The youngest pup near her wagged its tail. To it she said, "He never did tell me about the change of worlds."

She called to the dogs to follow her, but they did not. All seemed content to rest there at John Stink's side.

They did not come home that day. Effie waited to feed them, but they did not come. She slept alone in John Stink's house that night. Without him it was emptier than before. The dogs wandered in the next morning, one or two at a time. They ate and left. All day long they came and went. That evening Effie walked the three miles to visit John Stink's grave.

The dogs sat around the wooden structure. Seeing her, they jumped up and ran to her, pounced on her, and then they returned to sit down again. Their behavior baffled her. When she left the site, she tried to coax them home with her. Again they stayed.

Their strange behavior continued for two more days. Finally, when the animals came in to eat on the last day, she followed them back to the grave. She wrapped herself in a woolen shawl for the cool late evening and silently trailed behind the dogs.

The dogs sat on the ground when they arrived at the mound. She stood back, behind them, though they knew she was there. They looked at her from time to time and wagged their tails.

Effie sat down too, leaning against a fence post that marked the boundaries of the land. "They're waiting," she said aloud. "But what are they waiting for?"

She was there all night. One of the whining dogs woke her at dawn. She shook her shawl and wrapped herself snugly and went to sleep again. Later the warming sun woke her.

The dogs were all whining and pacing around John Stink's burial mound. One of them was standing on its hind legs and was pawing at a narrow opening between the nailed boards. With their front paws the other dogs were digging the dirt around the mound.

Effie watched in amazement and fear. In a frenzy, the dogs whined louder than ever. Walking to them, she tried to calm them. They continued to whine. She thought she heard something stir under their high-pitched cries, a movement of some kind. It came from inside the mound. She didn't know what to think and was afraid.

The dogs continued to dig, trying to open the boards. Realizing what had happened, she quickly ran to where one of the dogs was pawing. She began to pull away the dirt with her hands. Aloud she said, "What have I done to the Old Man? What have I done?"

She pulled one of the planks loose. Then she moved other planks. The dogs slipped through the boards. Inside the mound, they made excited cries and seemed to be jumping up and down.

She leaned over the boards and looked inside. Light seeped through the boards. She could not see anything but the dogs. When she called them, they came to her. John Stink's eyes glittered at her. She crawled inside and touched his hand. He was alive.

They walked home together. John Stink wore his black blanket with its red and green ribbons pulled around him. Effie's plaid shawl was draped over her shoulders. The dogs followed.

The white doctor was the first to learn of John Stink's resurrection. When Effie told him that John Stink had been unconscious before, he told her that this kind of thing did happen. It was rare, but it did happen.

John Stink's first appearance in town after that caused a commotion. The people whispered loudly, detesting him more than ever because of his resurrection.

It was then that they began to call him John Stink. They laughed among themselves, pleased with the name they gave him. They said that the dead did stink after a time, and he stunk most of all. They claimed that he talked to the spirits a lot after his resurrection. Effie acknowledged that John Stink did talk to himself a great deal, and he carried on long conversations with his dogs.

John Stink lived to be a very old man. Effie watched

him every day of that time. When he really did die, Effie waited and made sure that this time he was really gone before she let him be carried out to the burial site again.

He left her his dirt-floor house, where she lived the rest of her life. She had a wooden floor put in and added on to the house. Then she borrowed a child named Millie from a cousin with numerous children. Effie's house was complete now, rearing the child within John Stink's old home.

After Sunday school one morning, Millie came in the house and told Effie, "Grandma, at Sunday school they said Jesus was resurrected. He died and came alive again. I hate for you to die, Grandma, if I knew you could never come alive again."

Effie Grayeyes looked up from the quilt she was patching. She said, "There is no death, Millie. There is only a change of worlds."

Then she took Millie's hand. Effie led Millie toward the weathered mound where John Stink lay. As they walked she said, "Did I ever tell you about the change of worlds?"

Millie looked at Effie and said, "No, Grandma."

Effie's eyes sparkled, and she began, "Well, over twenty years ago, I buried an old bowlegged man called John Stink...."

# THE DEVIL
# AND
# SISTER LENA

*L*ena was a religious woman. She attended church at every opportunity even though an ancient tribal belief had been deeply instilled in her. She did not forsake "the old way" as she called it, and she taught both ways to the grandchild in her care. From the time it was a baby, she carried her not only to a variety of churches, but to the "Indian doings" as well. The churches dotted the hills, and Lena knew each church that sat near her family's allotted land. She had lived there for three-quarters of a century, her lifetime.

Lena's faith in all the denominations baffled and angered the pastors of the little country church-houses. For she was not the only one like that; there were other Indian people who were the same. The ministers decided then that the Indian flock were like children who had simple minds and led simple lives. Painstakingly, theology was explained to each of these potential converts, but patience was sorely tried on Lena. The preachers' frustration was held in check to simmer under Sunday smiles.

Lena attended each church erratically. Her absence and presence were duly noted on the rolls kept by the different congregations while she divided up the Sundays equally between churches. One by one, the pastors approached Lena to ask the same question. "Sister Lena, do you know what you are doing? All these churches you been agoing to... they ain't the same."

Lena pursed her lips. The wrinkles in her face settled into a hint of a smile. She nodded her scarfed head. "I'm gonna church. Be with Jesus."

"But Sister Lena," the pastors went on to say, "these churches don't all believe the same way."

Lena's sunken eyes widened. "Oh?" she asked with a naive smile.

Each pastor answered, "No. You see, Sister Lena, we have different rules we go by. We believe that God wants us to live in a certain way, and it's very different from the way those people in other churches live. Otherwise, we'd all be alike. Wouldn't make much difference what church we went to."

Lena sat for a while and looked into her grandchild's eyes. Then she looked at the church pastor she spoke to and said, "Ever since I a little girl, some peoples, they tole me that. But it don't matter. It's alla same."

In a state of exasperation, the preachers would say, "No, it's not the same, Sister Lena. You don't understand."

Lena would then purse her lips and nod her head again. "It's alla same. Yes, it is. Alla same. *You* don't understand."

Often Lena's response would end the conversation there. But one time a boyish preacher visited Lena's home to "try to talk some sense into her dense ole head," as he himself said. He wore a black suit and tie, even though the sun was unbearable that day.

"Save your soul, Sister Lena," he said outside her

house. "You getting old. Someday soon now, you going to die."

Lena's face settled into a playful smile again. She looked into the hills. She answered, "Face death ever day I live. Ever thing dies. It does. Shouldn't come as no surprise." As she talked, a mosquito landed on her wrist. She slapped it. She went on, "It happens like that. One day, you walking round and round. Next day you dead like this one here. Life's gone out. Them's the way things are. Don't worry bout that. Boy, you sceered to die?"

The preacher's pink face became red. Lena couldn't tell if he was angry or not. "No, I'm not scared to die!" he said. "I'm worried about you. Me, I'm saved. You...you going to burn in Hell unless you're saved. And then the Devil will rejoice. He's won!" He wiped his red face with a damp, limp handkerchief.

Lena's grandchild had been playing in the distance, crawling around in the dirt for some time. She came running to Lena then. Her face dripped with sweat. She said, "Grandma, looky here." She held her hand up to Lena.

Lena answered her, "Not now, baby. This man here, he's been trying to say something." The grandchild sat on the bench beside the preacher, her fingers clutched together.

The preacher continued louder than before. "As I was saying, Sister Lena, Hell is hot. You'll burn for eternity. Do you know how long that is?"

Lena wiped the child's face with the printed skirt of her faded dress. "It's lotta lifetimes. Too many to count. Too long to remember," she said. Her smile was gone and her voice was wistful. Thoughtfully, she looked at her gray house that once was white, then back to her grandchild again.

The preacher feared he'd lost her attention. He added quickly, "Don't give the Devil that chance to rejoice, Sister! He's evil! And Hell is hot!" He took off his suit jacket and threw it beside him as if to emphasize what he said.

Lena studied the tall, lanky white preacher with the sweat rolling down his neck. She was definitely interested in what he said, he could tell. His chest puffed out a bit to think he'd done it, scared some sense into her. Then she said, "Oklahoma must be like Hell a lot. It's sure hot!" The preacher was momentarily speechless. Lena continued. "The Debil? Well, you right bout him, preacher. I heered stories bout him. Seen him once too. Know what he looks like."

The preacher deflated like a punctured balloon. "Sister Lena," he enunciated each syllable angrily, "You don't know what the Devil looks like! What are you talking about?"

Lena rose from the upside-down can she sat on and walked to the preacher. Face to face with her, he saw the wrinkles in her face shift around as she bent to him and said, "Lissen here, I know." She whispered to the excited man, "He looks like you. Yes, he does. The Debil does. Looks jest like you."

His face went through several contortions before he was able to speak coherently. Lena's grandchild watched him go through the range of emotions. He blurted out several words. Lena knew two languages and couldn't make out what he said in either one of them. She wondered if he knew himself what he said. When he had calmed down somewhat, he told Lena, "Sister Lena, you're trying my patience."

Lena herself was patient with him as he recovered control. Eventually he wore a tight strained smile and managed to ask, "Why do you come to church anyway, Sister Lena? Do you believe in God?"

Lena answered without hesitation. "Because alla

these peoples, they ask me to come. Sides, I like it. Jesus I like. The songs, too."

The preacher shook his head and seemed to understand. He asked, "What do you know about God or Jesus?"

"Not too much. Jest what I heered over yonder in church," she admitted cheerfully.

He became more confident then and boldly said, "I hear you people don't have religion. Don't believe in God or Jesus."

For the first time in their conversation, Lena's mouth clamped shut. Her lips pursed tightly. She looked at him with open distrust and sat down again on the makeshift chair. She looked at the girl and said, "I'll tell you what I can. We don't got Jesus. We got something else. It's ever thing. Hard to sit and talk bout it. Can't say it in so many words. So we sing, we dance. What we have is a mystery. Don't got answers for it and don't understand it. But it's all right. Jest live right in it. Side by side."

"You talking superstition now Sister Lena," the preacher said. "Ain't nothing to it. That's what's wrong with you people. Better put that stuff behind you. For the sake of your grandchild there, if nothing else." He pointed at the little girl who watched his every move.

Lena answered him. "Thank you, preacher, but we came this far. Us peoples. Been looking out for ourselves. Came this far since the beginning. This girl's gonna know jest how things are."

When the preacher stood to leave, Lena's face was bright as she promised, "We see you at church come Sunday, preacher." He scowled while Lena giggled and the child waved.

When the preacher's car rolled between the hills, Lena turned to her grandchild and asked, "Now what is it?"

The little girl held up her hand and showed three

little eggs. "Them's snake eggs, baby," Lena said. "Take them back and put them where they was."

That evening when the day's work was done, Lena and the grandchild sat outside in the breeze. Lena asked, "Baby, you put them snake eggs back like I tole you?" The grandchild nodded. Darkness descended upon them while Lena talked. "They's lotsa snakes hereabouts, baby." Her voice threw the words through the hills. "Got to watch. Some of these snakes, they's harmless. And some's poison. Got to know which is which. Those green and black snakes, they nothing. They mind their own business. Let them pass. Leave all of them alone. My father, he tole me, daughter—you can't always see them snakes, but you gonna know when you git bit."

For nights after, Lena's words bounced back to the child's ears until she knew them as well as she knew each line in her grandmother's face and hands. But for then, she sat and remembered all the snakes she'd met in the hills and creeks. She knew that even as she sat with Lena there, snakes hung in the trees around them, hissing with long and delicate tongues as they did when she climbed the trees to examine them. That very morning when she collected eggs from the chicken coop, her chubby fingers groped a blacksnake instead of eggs. It had stolen them. The eggshells were completely intact, with tiny holes drilled into them where the snake sucked the eggs out.

Lena was saying, "Got to watch your step. Look round and lissen!" The child nodded her head in the darkness. Her face wore a serious expression.

The star patterns slowly slid across the sky. The grandchild lifted her finger and began to count the stars. Then she remembered the preacher and turned to Lena. She asked Lena, "That whiteman was sure mad at us today, huh?"

Lena's silhouette nodded under the stars.

"Why, Grandma? How come he acted mean with us?" the girl wanted to know.

Lena began to unravel the girl's braids. "Not his fault, baby," she said. "He's jest young. And he thinks he knows ever thing."

"You shoulda tole him bout things, Grandma," the grandchild said, as she hugged the old lady protectively.

Lena squeezed the chubby arms clinging around her and said, "Wouldn't do no good, baby. He don't lissen. Don't hear the wind and the rain, the trees, and the grass. Don't hear it, the voice inside the mystery." Lena pulled the pins out of her white hair, and it fell free over her shoulders.

She stood and stretched. The girl grabbed Lena's shirts and followed to the heavy metal bed with broken springs where they slept in good weather. Lena opened the quilts. She and her grandchild lay down to rest.

"They purty, huh, Grandma?" the young one asked and pointed to the twinkling stars.

"Stars is pretty all right," Lena agreed.

"Hey Grandma," the child lay on her belly and looked at Lena. "Is ever thing purty like stars?"

Lena's eyes glittered much like the stars above her. She answered, "Baby, it depends on how you look at it. They's somethings in the world what's not too pretty. They's people, mostly."

The child put a chubby hand on Lena's face as she told her grandmother, "You purty, Grandma. Got eyes like stars."

Lena laughed and said, "We can't see ever thing what's in the world, baby. They's lotsa things in the world sides jest what we see."

The child was immediately curious. She moved closer to her grandmother. Lena straightened the blankets saying, "We not the only ones what lives. Us peoples knows. Some others maybe think they's the only ones what live. And too, things ain't always what they look like. We walk round and round, moving through life. Life so big. It mysterious and it all round us, ever where. Lotsa times though, us peoples can't see what's round us. It gonna be there though, sure enough."

Lena's and the grandchild's forms fused with darkness. Both were motionless while Lena spoke, "Out there, they's a lot what lives and moves. Us peoples knows it because it touches us. Then us peoples seem like little things next to it. It big and mysterious. Yes, lotsa times us peoples feel it, if we want to or not. It jest touches us, and us peoples thinks we's part of it."

Lena tapped the child lightly on a wrist, and the child felt it with her entire body. "That's how it is," Lena said to her. "Jest like that. That's how come we knows they's other things in the world sides only what we see. Us peoples been thinking this since the first day. Don't hardly talk bout it much tween ourselves. Can't say much bout something what's plain as day. But you jest a baby, so I tole you. Gonna help you out a little so you can go a long ways."

The little girl's eyes darted about in the darkness, exploring it for what she did not see in it. The child's thoughts went to the preacher again. Then the girl bit her tongue but could not stop a question. "What does the Devil look like, Grandma?"

Lena rolled to her side and looked her grandchild in the face. She told the girl, "Well, some says he's red and has horns and a long tail. But they's others who says he's handsome and can make hisself look like anything he wants to look like."

"Is the Devil a man?" the grandchild asked.

Lena watched airplane lights flicker in the sky. It was a while before she replied. "I don't know, baby. Maybe. Some Indian peoples though says the Debil is a whiteman." Lena coughed as she spoke. The words came spitting out. The girl thought that Lena smiled when she said that, but could not know for sure in the dark. Everything was quiet, except for the plane that plowed through the stars. Just when the girl thought Lena was asleep, Lena said, "Got to watch for him, baby. Look and lissen, like you do round snakes. Jest pick your steps round him."

"Who you talking bout, Grandma?" the girl asked. "The Devil?"

Lena did laugh then in a soft voice. She promised, "Baby, the time's a coming. You gonna see. I gonna be there though. See you through it. But baby, after that, you on your own." Lena squeezed the girl's plump hand and held onto it until both slept soundly. Around them, the wind gently blew and the trees and the grass danced in the darkness.

Three years had passed. Lena's grandchild was eight. She was thinner, but her eyes had grown to twice their size. Lena and the girl sat on their broken bed and surveyed the camp in the evening.

About three hundred canvas tents were scattered along the creekbanks. A few cars, mostly 1950 models, were parked beside the tents. Wagons were more numerous. Horses grazed in the pasture beyond the narrow creek that wound about the camp on three sides. Pecan and cottonwood trees shaded the tents with filtered sunlight during the hottest part of the day. That day it had reached 105 in the shade. In the evening it cooled though and must have been in the lower 90s then. Lena fanned herself with one of the girl's comic books.

They had eaten, and a small cooking fire sent tendrils of smoke up into the trees. It hung there without any breeze to dissipate it. Around them other small cooking fires burned, and the sound of people's voices drifted back and forth across the creek. Something dropped out of the tree limbs over them and landed at Lena's and the girl's feet. It was a twig. The girl looked up toward the tree but could not see anything in the shadows.

"It's a tree snake," Lena told her. "Harmless. After a big old nest up yonder. Been up there for days. Since we got here."

"How do you know, Grandma?" the girl asked Lena.

Lena answered, "I seen him. Spotted him as soon as we got here. Ain't gonna bother us none."

Bells began to jingle in the tents near them and far away. Drumbeats came down the creekbanks to them. Lena and the girl could see the men who would dance shake their bright bustles and hang them on the tents and wagons. The bustles looked like shields from a distance.

Lena went into the tent, calling her grandchild after her. She helped the girl put on a black shirt with rows of satin and silk ribbons at the hem and down the front of the skirt. The ribbons were brilliant colors. Lena pulled a dark pink satin shirt over the girl's head on top of the skirt. Ribbons ran across the shoulders in the front and back of the blouse. Above these ribbons were metal ornaments about the size of quarters scattered randomly across the top of the blouse. Lena tied several bright scarves at the girl's neck and hung several strands of black glass beads over the scarves. The beads were heavy and swung down below the girl's waist. Next, Lena stuck some beads into the girl's braids. The girl was ready when she slipped on a pair of black moccasins. As the two left the tent, Lena handed the girl a dark pink shawl with long fringes for use when the girl danced.

In the next tent an old man sang to himself. Drumbeats floated down the creek and became muted in the trees as Lena and the girl walked through the encampment on their way to the evening's dance. At two tents they stopped to visit relatives. By the time they arrived, activities were underway.

Lena had brought her own metal folding chair from their tent. She unfolded it and put it behind the white painted benches the dancers used. Then Lena settled down to visit with a woman next to her. Half a dozen men dancers sat in front of Lena on the white benches. The girl took a place on the bench beside the men dancers. She had decided on arrival that something was peculiar about the evening, but was unable then to say exactly what it was. Her large eyes went around the arena, over the dancers and other tribal people there.

The sun hid itself behind the hill where the agency building was constructed. A string of electric lightbulbs that circled the dance arena suddenly lit up. An announcer at the speaker's stand welcomed the crowd. His voice went out over the public address system. "*Aho!* We greet all our relatives and guests tonight. Welcome to the first night of our annual gathering." The girl knew that his speech would be long. She became restless. Lena gave her some coins for a soft drink. She disappeared into the standing crowd behind the rows of folding chairs that people had brought and set up. The girl took her time getting her refreshment and returning. She could hear each speaker through the microphone, and when the drum began to pound and the songs started, she headed back. She leaned on Lena's arm and tried to figure out what was so different about the night.

A few dancers were dancing in a round dance line. They moved counterclockwise around the arena in a shuffling step. Fringes swayed brilliantly under the string of light bulbs. Men in furry hats or feathered headdresses danced with more energy than did the women. The line bobbed up and down as the dancers moved around the arena. The girl laid the pink shawl over her arm and joined the dancers at the end of the line. She looked much like the other dancers. As the girl danced, she studied the faces of the observers. The girl saw that Lena watched her approvingly and noticed, too, that Lena watched someone else. Lena's face fell briefly into a frown, her eyes narrowed and her lips pursed. Then she looked at the girl and smiled calmly across the dance arena.

After that dance ended, the girl returned to her seat. Lena was bent toward her neighbor. The woman was whispering something into Lena's ear. The girl then realized there was no laughter, or joking, or teasing conversation that usually accompanied these gatherings. That was what was different! Everyone spoke in whispers. The girl's eyes moved from Lena to others who all were whispering to each other around the arena.

Another dance began. The crowd around the girl was murmuring among themselves and pointed to someone in the newly formed line of dancers. The girl wanted to know who it was. The beginning of the dance line was approaching. The girl quickly counted nearly forty dancers. They passed in front of her in a snakelike line. The girl studied the people sitting around her again. No one sang along with the singers as was common, or tapped their fingers or feet to the drum. The people were rigid in their seats and leaned toward the dancers. The line danced by in front of her. The girl watched the last dancer pass. Then a buzz of whispers filled the air.

"Grandma," she tugged at Lena's taffeta sleeve, "What's going on?" The girl's voice was loud over the whispers. She sat on the bench and leaned back to Lena. Lena's eyes sparkled like the black glass beads the girl wore. Lena put a finger over her own lips and motioned the girl to be silent and watch. The girl obeyed and sat quietly through the dance, watching the strange behavior around her.

Another song started. The head dancers were the

first to rise. The man moved out first. The feathers on his head and arms began to shake and swirl. The woman was dressed in pale yellows. Her dance was a startling contrast to the man's. She was demure, dignified, and restrained in her steps. Her feet were soft and made no sound or impression on the ground. She held her head high and straight. In her right hand, she carried a large eagle wing fan. Other dancers rose to join the head dancers after a few seconds.

The girl searched the group of dancers for her favorite clown. He was a humorous old man who pranced and paraded before the ladies when he danced. He was so vain. He always donned mixed-up dancing clothes that were forbidden for other dancers but were his trademark. All the undesirable qualities in a dancer is what he represented. He brought the tribal people much joy with his foolish dancing ways. Yes, the clown was there sitting on a bench, but he had not moved the whole evening. The girl thought that very strange!

Another dance started. It was a two-step, adapted from the white community. The head dancers led the column of dancers again. This time, though, several dancers seemed undecided as to whether or not they would dance. A few did begin to dance but then abruptly returned to the benches and sat stiffly down. About a dozen couples continued to dance. Most of them wore confused expressions on their faces.

The people sitting with Lena watched someone in the file of dancers. Their whispers were loud, and the girl tried to make out what they said. They spoke in Indian and it was all muffled. Lena frowned and pursed her lips. A tense feeling was in the air. The people seemed to have gone from apprehension to anger and indignation.

The girl knew most of the dancers either through kinship or by their dancing reputation. The first eight couples were all adults. The young people were next.

Each lady who danced wore a shawl over her street clothes or dance dress, but a few of the men danced in street wear and cowboy boots.

The girl squinted her eyes to block out the glare of the light bulbs. She saw that not all the men were Indian. Three were not. The girl was related to most of the Indian men. One of the whitemen was married into the tribe, so he was considered one of them.

Suddenly, Lena grabbed the girl's arm and pulled the girl onto her lap. The girl was too old for this, and Lena was so small. Lena hadn't held her this way for a long time. The girl soon saw why this was done.

An old lady, older than Lena, made her way toward them from the crowd behind. The old lady stopped beside the girl and Lena. The old lady's eyes were cloudy as she laid them on the tribal people around her. She looked at Lena and nodded to her. Lena returned the gesture. The old lady looked at the girl. "Hi, Grandma," the girl said without hesitation, as she did to all the old women. The old lady paid the girl no attention. The girl thought the old lady's cloudy eyes burned like embers for an instant. Then the old lady turned away from the girl and watched the dancers. The old lady's presence was observed carefully by other tribal members.

The old lady watched one of the whitemen. He was unfamiliar to the girl. He danced with one of the tribe's young women. The woman was of French and Indian ancestry. She had inherited her great-grandfather's French name and his fair complexion. She wore a red dance dress, and her partner was in a gray cowboy suit with a white cowboy hat. Lena's grandchild thought this whiteman quite handsome.

The old lady at the girl's side muttered something to herself. She turned to Lena and looked down at her. She said only one word to Lena. The girl had never heard it before. The old lady said it softly; it was almost a whisper.

Her body seemed to deflate and shrink with the pronounce-
ment of the word. The old lady's cloudy eyes sternly
looked at the dancing cowboy once more. The dance had
ended. The cloudy eyes followed as he escorted the
young woman to a chair across the arena. Everyone
watched him.

The girl in Lena's arms watched the old lady as she
turned back into the crowd without saying another word
and disappeared into the darkness that hovered over the
electric light bulbs and all around.

BOOM! BOOM! The drum made muffled tones and a
high-pitched man's voice began to sing. Other singers,
male and female, soon joined in, continuing the evening
dance. But there was commotion in the speaker's stand.

Lena's gaze had never left the whiteman on the far
side of the arena. Lena pointed to him and held her finger
in front of the girl's eyes, so the child could see him. He
was in the company of another young woman. They
casually strolled to the dance area. He was much taller
than she as he danced at her side, clumsy and a bit out of
step with the other men. His partner, on the other hand,
was graceful and small. Members of the tribe were rising
from their seats to stand and watch this couple. Children
stood on tiptoe and pushed people and clothing away
that blocked their view.

As the whiteman and his young woman danced in
front of Lena and the girl, the people actually pointed at
him openly. Whispers were louder than before. The
people were definitely angry. Suddenly, the drum stopped
in the middle of a song! The few dancers quickly dis-
persed.

The whiteman led the young woman to her chair.
The girl, still in Lena's arms, saw the young woman's
mother meet her daughter and the whiteman halfway
there. The mother pulled on the daughter's arm, away
from the man. The young woman's face wore surprise

and embarrassment at her mother's behavior, but the daughter surrendered and left with her mother. The whiteman simply moved on, acting as if he was totally unaware of the commotion that he caused. He stopped in front of two more young women, and by their smiles, even Lena's grandchild knew he would stay there for a while.

Several minutes passed. The singers had abandoned the drum. Static came over the public address system. Then a voice called through the microphone, "My relatives, we are going to cancel the rest of the evening's activities. Gather your families and return to your tents. Remain there for the rest of the night." The words hung in the air with the camp smoke and darkness. The announcement was repeated twice, once in English and once in the tribal tongue. People began to move toward their tents. Lena folded her chair as she talked to others in barely audible tones.

The girl saw that a crowd collected around the whiteman in the gray suit; it was made up mostly of admiring young women. The old lady who appeared out of the darkness earlier was then approaching this group. The old lady momentarily stood beneath a wavering yellow light bulb that cast an unearthly glow on her. She put a withered hand on one of the women who stood on the outskirts of the group. The old lady said something to the young woman. The young woman's smooth face became contorted. She turned and fled.

A few men were helping the people leave. The people at the dance area had thinned by half, but the remainder were moving out slowly. The microphone screeched and came alive. A breathless male voice said something in Indian, then in English. It said, "My relatives, the Devil is among us tonight. Take your families to your tents! Stay there!" The people began to scurry.

The whiteman with his crowd of women admirers paid no attention to the loudspeaker. He walked toward Lena and her grandchild. The girl darted toward him before Lena knew it. Only four or five feet away from him, the girl's curiosity had peaked. She rushed in to have a look at him. The top of his white felt hat was visible. She squeezed through the ladies surrounding him. His clothing was within reach. She could not see his face. The girl's hand went out to touch him. Just as her fingers opened, the girl was yanked away from him by the neck of her blouse. Lena swatted the girl twice and led her to their tent. All the way to the tent, Lena did not release the hold on the girl's blouse. The girl thought that she would choke.

Lena pulled the girl into their tent and lit the coal oil lamp. She dumped the girl into bed, dance clothes and all. Then Lena blew out the lamp and sat a long time on the broken bed, beside the girl.

The girl lay there and listened to the camp. It made no sound. Its presence under the trees might never be known, she thought. There were no camp lights, no voices, no movement of any kind. The electric lightbulbs over the dance arena had been unplugged, and campfires had died. The only sound of life the girl heard was Lena's breathing and her own heart beating in the corner of their tent. The girl could not resist opening the tent flap Lena had closed. She looked outside at the dark, silent camp.

"What do you see?" Lena whispered into the girl's ear.

The girl answered, "Nothing, Grandma."

Lena's face turned toward the girl. Lena's eyes blinked and shone in the dark. She whispered, "Look again."

Lena woke the girl just after sunrise. "Gonna pull the tent down and go on home, baby," she said. The girl was momentarily disappointed because she always liked these gatherings. Still dressed in last night's rumpled clothing, the girl went outside and looked around. The tent that had been next to them was already gone. Only a clear square piece of ground hinted that anything had been there. Other tents were being dismantled.

The girl went back inside the tent to change. She closed the tent flaps for privacy. Someone approached the side of the tent. A female voice said, "Sister Lena, will you have a way to get home, you and the girl?"

Lena answered, "Sent word this morning. We be gone by midday. Someone will come." Lena was cooking for the girl.

The voice said again, "Sister Lena, they found another one. That's three now." As the girl changed her clothing, she listened.

Lena sat down on the bench beside the table. The girl knew because the bench always squeaked under the slightest weight. Lena answered, "Don't come as no surprise. Who are they?"

The other voice said, "I don't know. They all danced with him, though. One simply did not wake this morning. One passed in the night. This one they are talking about now, but I really don't know the details. Do the details matter?"

The girl imagined that Lena was shaking her head, no.

The voice went on. "Well, Sister Lena, we're ready to leave, so I have to go now. I suppose you will want to help put these girls away?"

With her braids undone and her hair hanging loose, the girl came out of the tent. Lena was nodding to the caller.

"Well, baby, gonna eat now. Got lots to do. Be evening before we sit down again," Lena said.

The girl sat down at the table and spooned cereal

into her mouth. The tree leaves above the girl and Lena rustled. The girl looked up. A large black snake was wound around the overhanging limb. The girl made a face at it. She stuck out her tongue at it like the snakes often did to her. She laid down her spoon, looked at Lena, and asked, "How did you know, Grandma?"

Lena answered, "It's happened before. Seen some things before. Us peoples knows lotsa things. Jest keeps it to ourselves. Now, come on, eat. Be too hot to move soon."

"Like Hell?" the girl asked Lena.

Lena swallowed her cereal and said, "Looks to me like you learning, baby."

# APPARITIONS

$W$anda looked at the distorted reflections of herself and her mother as they passed in front of the store window wishing for a Maytag washing machine and a vacuum cleaner with at least six attachments, though their house had no throw rugs, let alone a thick carpet like the one shown in the store window. Wanda was shorter than her momma, and her mother was short alongside of the other promenading figures moving past the store window. There were other differences, too. Wanda's momma wore a black-and-white checkered housedress and long braids held together by a red rubberband. Wanda was a younger version of her mother in a cotton print dress and faded light blue tennis shoes. Wanda's momma wore moccasins over her flesh-colored stockings. The other figures, apparitions in the tinted store glass window, looked Wanda and her momma up and down as they passed the mother and daughter. The men wore summer suits and white shoes, while the women wore high-heeled shoes. Their coiffures were nestlike: a strand of hair never strayed out of place, even in the summer breeze.

Wanda turned away from the glass window to a woman standing beside her looking at something inside the display. Wanda looked her up and down. The woman wore spiked heels and a pink knitted dress. The red-brown nest was in place upon her head. Her lips were red, and her eyes were purple just above the lids. She carried a large handbag which she then raised to open. Wanda realized the woman was looking at herself in the window. The woman pulled out a chrome-colored tube and applied some more red to her mouth. Then the woman turned to Wanda and gazed at her for a few seconds. "Hi honey," the woman said. Wanda didn't answer. She just stared at the nest that was the woman's hair. The woman frowned and looked to Wanda's momma, who was counting change in a small beaded coin purse. The woman dug into her boxlike handbag again and stared tentatively at Wanda. Impulsively, she grabbed one of Wanda's hands and pressed a fifty-cent piece into it. Then she held her red lips tightly together in a straight horizontal line and marched off, her spiked heels clicking on the hot cement.

They were mostly quarters inside the coin purse. The little pouch bulged out when Wanda's momma snapped the top shut. She put the coin purse inside her housedress pocket and the weight of the quarters made the pocket fabric pull down on one side of it. Then Wanda's momma took out a headscarf, neatly folded, from the other pocket of her housedress. At one corner of the scarf was a knot which she began to untie. Wanda watched.

There were one dollar bills in the knot. There were four of them. Wanda's momma lifted her eyes to Wanda with a smile and said, "Over seven dollars, Wanda. It's more than enough."

Wanda held out the fifty-cent piece to her momma. Wanda's momma said, "Where'd you get that?"

"That woman who was here," Wanda said.

"Well, come on, Wanda," her mother said. "We have to get back home to fix your daddy's supper because he's got to work again tonight." She pushed Wanda's fifty-cent piece away.

Wanda followed her mother down the street amidst the clicking of high heels and the brush of tailored summerwear. Wanda watched the apparitions in the brown and pink-tinted store window glass. The apparitions moved about curiously on the smooth glassy surface, entering one side and disappearing on the opposite side.

The huge sign hanging from a bank building corner said that it was three o'clock and 92 degrees. Following that came a long message about investing in certificates and saving for the future. Wanda did not read it, though she knew most of the words. She was in the third grade.

She plodded along after her mother. At the department store, Wanda's mother stopped and waited for Wanda to enter.

It was cold inside the store. Again, Wanda followed her mother to a counter that said LAY-AWAYS HERE.

"Yes," a young woman with horned rimmed glasses said to Wanda's momma.

"Well," Wanda's momma said, "I came to pay off my lay-away." Wanda's momma's voice was naturally quiet. She was soft-spoken.

The woman behind the counter did not know that. She said harshly, "You'll have to speak up if you want help around here." She looked Wanda and her mother up and down, her eyes lingering on Wanda's momma's braids and moccasins.

Wanda's momma grimaced slightly, but she raised her voice to accommodate the woman behind the counter. She said, "I came to pay off my lay-away."

The woman frowned and turned away to search a stack of files. She found the right group of files and asked, "Name?"

Wanda's momma asked, "What?"

The store clerk turned and put a hand on her bony hip and said very loudly, "I asked you your name. Can't you hear?" Other customers nearby lifted their eyes curiously to the store clerk and Wanda's momma.

Wanda's momma answered, "My name is Marie Horses."

The store clerk answered, "Horses? It figures." She quickly pulled out a yellow sheet of paper and said, "You owe $4.50 on that."

Marie Horses untied the handkerchief knot and laid the four dollar bills on the counter. The store clerk watched incredulously. Marie Horses then took out two quarters from her coin purse and laid them down.

The store clerk disappeared through a curtain hanging behind her and returned carrying a package. She set it down before Wanda and her mother.

Wanda's momma said, "I'll be putting something else in lay-away today." She waited to see if the woman had heard, but the clerk gave no indication that she knew Wanda and her momma were alive.

Wanda's momma led the way again down the tiled aisles to the shoe department. They passed plastic shower curtains and towels hanging from brightly colored plastic rods. These things Marie Horses touched. In the fabric section, she stopped and went to touch some white satin cloth. It was smooth under her fingers, and she lay the cloth against her face. She smiled with delight at the feel of the satin on her face.

Once in the shoe section of the store, the two people, mother and daughter, sat down in low, orange chairs. This part of the store was carpeted. Wanda's momma reached down and ran her fingers over the carpet texture.

The man who came out of another curtain at the back of this store section was quite tall and middle-aged. His eyes were on the package Marie Horses carried. He said, "Can I help you? If not, those chairs are for paying customers." When he said *paying*, he said *PAY-YING*. He'd had it with people coming in to sit down for a few minutes to cool off.

"Yes," Wanda's mother answered. "The girl needs shoes. See?" Marie Horses showed the tear in one of Wanda's tennis shoes. She said, "I sewed it twice. Bloodied myself with the needle. Can't sew it anymore."

The man measured Wanda's foot in a metal contraption. He studied the measurement, then turned to Marie Horses. "How much money you want to spend? The amount of money you can spend is going to rule out certain things. How much money you have?"

Marie Horses blushed ever so slightly. The man did not notice. She said, "It's all right. I have money. I'm going to put them on lay-away for the girl."

He was looking at a rack of merchandise behind him, and he pulled a pink tennis shoe off the display. Along with that, he pulled a white plastic shoe with buckles. Then he disappeared into the curtain again.

He carried several pairs still in boxes when he returned. He deposited all the boxes in front of Wanda.

Wanda lifted her foot with the white sock so that he could slip one of the shoes on her. He told her, "Stand on it." Wanda stood in the stiff shoe.

He felt her left toe, and then he put his hand on her left calf. He kept his hand there. He said, "How does that shoe fit you?" Wanda didn't say anything. He moved his hand to her knee and held her there. Wanda's dress hem covered his hand. He told Wanda to sit down again and he put the other shoe on Wanda's other foot. This time he placed both of his hands on Wanda's legs. His hands were on Wanda's knees. "Those shoes fit all right?" he asked.

Marie Horses sat studying the shoes, not aware of the place the salesman's hands lingered. Wanda would not look at her mother's face. The salesman moved his hands up to Wanda's thighs, and all the time he talked about the shoes Wanda wore. Finally his hands came out of Wanda's dress, and he pulled off the shoes.

The salesman turned to Marie Horses now, giving her his full attention. He said, "Ma'am, if you're going to put these shoes on lay-away, you'd better go see the lady at the Department to see if it will be all right. Me and the girl here will keep trying the shoes on until we find a pair that fits."

Marie Horses thought about this and said, "The lady knows already."

The salesman frowned and said, "Well, no one told me. Someone will have to tell me before I let you carry these shoes off." Marie Horses turned red in the face. She got out of her chair and padded down the tiled aisles again in her moccasined feet.

Wanda wanted to run after Marie Horses, but the salesman glared at her, and one of his hands tightly pinched one of her knees. The other hand dug into the flesh behind her other knee. He released one hand with a silent warning and took another shoe out of a tan shoebox.

Wanda looked around. There was no one else in this part of the store.

Again, the man pushed Wanda's foot into the plastic shoe. Then he forced the other foot into the other shoe. Again, he told her to stand, while his hands moved from her knees to her thighs. He was talking to her. Wanda didn't know what he said. Then his hands went higher to Wanda's pink underpants. His fingers jabbed her. Still he talked about the shoes. Wanda tried to move away from him. He grabbed her viciously on one of her thighs, and his eyes glared into hers. His other hand slipped beneath Wanda's underwear.

The closest saleslady was at a counter a few aisles over, straightening clothes that customers had ruffled through and then not purchased. Marie Horses was walking toward Wanda and the salesman, but she was quite a distance away. Wanda raised her hand to motion to Marie Horses. The salesman understood what Wanda was trying to do. He pulled on her thighs, and Wanda sat down hard on the chair before she realized it. Marie Horses was then only a few feet away. The salesman left the shoes on Wanda and stood beside her. His face became blank and expressionless. He held his hands clasped together behind his back. Wanda watched him. He looked like the other apparitions in the store glass windows outside. His nice summerwear rustled when he moved, and his white shoes made no sound on the carpeted floor.

Marie Horses said to him, "The lady said for you to bring the shoes over to her when you are ready." To Wanda Marie Horses said, "You like those shoes, honey?" Wanda didn't reply.

The salesman said, "Those shoes fit her fine."

Wanda took off the shoes by herself and wrapped them in the tissue paper in the shoebox. She still had the fifty-cent piece in her hand. The salesman took the box to the lady at the counter. He said, "Doris, got a ticket for you to write up over here." The lady he spoke to was the same one who had dealt with Wanda and Marie Horses earlier. When Doris didn't respond to him, Marie Horses told him, "That lady can't hear too good. You have to speak up to her." The shoe salesman left Wanda and Marie Horses there with the shoebox.

Eventually, Doris came over to them and prepared

the sales ticket. She collected $3.50 from Wanda's momma. Then the two, mother and daughter, left the store and went out into a hot burst of wind.

Wanda was quiet, looking at her mother from time to time with a hard-to-read expression on her face. Marie Horses noticed. She asked Wanda, "You want to spend your fifty-cent piece before we go home?" Wanda looked at the shiny coin in her sweaty hand. She shook her head no and let the coin drop through her fingers. It rolled down the sidewalk past Marie Horses' moccasins and stopped a few feet away with a ping. It glittered in the four o'clock sun. Wanda didn't retrieve it. Neither did Marie Horses. Their reflections went from store window to store window as they made their way out of town. After a few minutes, Marie Horses turned to Wanda and asked, "Honey, you like coming into town?"

"No," Wanda said emphatically.

"Me neither," Marie Horses said, and they walked on in silence.

# THE LAWS

*A* police car made its way down the street of evening shadows. The two occupants in the marked car flashed a spotlight on the sides of the street, the rows of beat-up houses. In one of the yellow-lit windows moved a tall gray figure. He bent toward the window to pull back the filmy curtain. "It's them two laws again, Momma," he said to his mother. She didn't answer him or seem surprised. She meticulously stitched two pieces of cloth together.

He watched as the black and white patrol car turned the corner at the end of the block. Then he spun around to the woman and said, "Them laws are anxious to hang any Indian they can git their hands on. Can't wait to see em with their eyes bulgin out and their tongues a waggin, kickin on the end of a rope. How come they been ridin round here lately, anyways? They never care what's happening down here... unless somebody over in town gits robbed and wants to pin the blame on some poor ole dumb Indian down here."

The woman didn't respond. Her fingers pulled the needle through the tiny even stitches.

The man disappeared into the back of the house. When he walked into the room again, his hair was slicked back. He was buttoning a new red-and-black checkered shirt. He smelled of aftershave lotion.

"Be back later, Momma," he said, and put a hand on the doorknob to leave. Then he went to the woman and rested his massive hands on her narrow shoulders. The top of her head glistened.

She lifted her head to look up at him. "Where you off to, Sonny?" she asked.

He looked her straight in the eye and said, "Nowhere, Momma, don't be worryin none, hear? It'll make you gray."

His mother unconsciously touched one hand to her dark hair with gray streaks in it. She smiled faintly and he left.

She placed her sewing things on the table beside her. Then she got up from the chair and looked out the window. No sign of the police car. Yellow light spilled out of the square windows in the houses across the street. Everything else was black.

She paced the length of the square room. Back and forth she walked, her arms folded over her bibbed apron. More than an hour passed. She found herself looking towards Sonny's room often. She paced more frantically.

Finally, she walked to his room with hesitant and measured steps. She pulled the cord that dangled under the lightbulb in the ceiling. The room lit. She stood beneath the dim light for a minute.

Sonny's room was just as it had always been. The army bed was roughly made. The dresser with the missing knobs still leaned against the back wall for support. Dirty clothes lay in a heap in a corner.

She didn't really know for what she searched. She

shrugged, sat down on the bed. Her fist pounded the pillow as she surveyed the room again. She kept hitting the pillow while her eyes went from the dirty clothes, to the dresser, up the lightbulb, to the foot of the bed, and then to her fist in the pillow. From under the rumpled pillow, from inside the pillow case, several rolls of banded bills slipped out.

She was dumbfounded, unable to speak or move. Like a statue, her body froze into that position she held. Her head slightly bowed, her shoulders drooped. At her right hand lay more money than she had ever seen all at once in her lifetime. She glared at the money for a long time with glazed eyes, trying to think. Then her small body moved. Her hands lifted to her eyes brimmed with tears, and she wiped them on her apron. Never in her wildest dreams did she think that Sonny's problems would escalate to this.

Sonny met two men waiting for him not far from his mother's house. In the night they greeted each other with a slap on the back. Their laughter carried through the night air.

Sallie had been sixteen years old when she bore Sonny, his daddy's pride and joy. Everything was good in life to the day her husband died. He had coughed and coughed. Finally the blood came up and he died. Tom told her before he died, "Sallie," he said, "if you need help keeping the boy on the right road, go to the tribe."

The first time she asked for help in raising the boy, she walked up to a group of old men who were telling each other whopping lies. She stood beside them until a silence fell and said aloud, "I wish I had help with Tom Hoop's boy. Someone to teach it right from wrong. Git onto it, fore it gits into no good. Poor thing, it don't have no father no more." From then on, the old men disciplined the boy. They lectured Sonny strong. A stern group, they didn't hesitate to raise their voices to the boy.. She didn't mind; the boy was coming along.

But one day one of the old men shoved the boy for stealing a folding dollar. Sallie's heart pained at the boy's punishment and got in the way. She took Sonny back again. The old men frowned when she claimed her child again. They studied each other. A couple of them spit tobacco on the ground. But they didn't say a word against or for the boy. Instead, they looked away from Sallie as she talked, until she finally left. Afterwards the old men left Sallie and Sonny alone. It had been nearly six years to the day that she had first asked for help from them when this happened. Sonny was thirteen now.

After that when Sonny did something wrong, Sallie's pride was too big. It would not permit her to go back to the tribe, to the old men, and say, "Here, take him. I was wrong."

Sonny married Liza Spotted Horse when he was twenty. He stayed with her just long enough to father a daughter. Sonny was drunk the day she was born and saw the child for the first time when he sobered up a few days later. By then Sonny had a white woman with big floppy breasts he admired for a while. She gave Sonny another daughter with gray eyes a few months after Liza's child was born. Liza took Sonny back after that, and in their reconciliation, he made another daughter.

Then he disappeared, went up north for a while to work on a railroad line. When Sonny came back about a year later, he brought another daughter-in-law for Sallie to meet. Her stomach was swollen out. She was painfully shy.

Angered, Sallie called Sonny into her small room. "Sonny," she said, "this is a bad thing to do! Making babies over here, over there! Only dogs do that, make puppies and then run off. Never see them again!"

Sonny looked hurt, but Sallie ignored the look on his face that she always gave in to and left him there alone to go hug the timid, little girl in the next room.

Sonny stayed close to home for the next few years. Sometimes he stayed with his women; at other times with Sallie. He worked off and on, doing construction for the white people in town.

At times Sonny seemed very content, but other times he cursed everything, from the weather to the women he knew.

Sallie pounded on the pane of glass in the window. A short heavy-set man peeked out. The door opened and Sallie ran in. She still wore her apron and had pulled it tightly around a bundle she clutched.

"What is it?" the man asked when he saw her pained face.

"Is Momma here?" she asked him.

He pointed to the door leading to another room. A woman with long thin braids entered. She looked at Sallie and said, "What is it?"

Sallie opened the apron. Bills dropped on the kitchen table.

Sallie's mother and stepfather looked at the bills. For a few minutes, neither of them moved.

"Sonny," Sallie's mother said. Sallie didn't know if it was a question or not. The man just sighed.

Sallie said, "I don't know what to do or where to turn. I wish there was some help somewhere."

The man cleared his throat, told Sallie what to do, what he would do, and what Sonny had to do. Sallie nodded, her eyes misting again.

Then Sallie's stepfather took a paper grocery sack from a kitchen drawer. With a broad swipe, he swept the money into it, pulled on his jacket and black hat with a long feather in it. The old man went out the door. Sallie watched his figure go into the darkness, her heart pounding rapidly as the police car crawled toward him.

*"These damn Indians stink,"* one cop said to the other. His hair was orange and stood on end. His face was splashed with brown freckles which moved around when he changed expressions.

His partner steered the car down the street and looked out the corner of his eyes to the orange-haired man. The driver said, "They ain't all bad. Why I grew up with em. They ain't all bad. They got their own ways; they take care of their own."

The orange-haired cop looked at his partner in disgust. He said, "Aw man, they're always raisin all kinds of hell! Take that robbery in town. I bet these Indians is to blame for it. They don't have no kind of rule, brought up lyin and cheatin all the time. The owner said himself that it was an Indian who done it. Had to be! They're the only ones who work for him. He's too cheap to pay anybody else."

Sallie's stepfather stood outside the highway patrol station, three miles from home. Several patrol cars were parked in front of the white metal building. He walked without a sound to one of the cars and looked inside. The doors were all locked. He moved to the next one. A front door was unlocked, the windows rolled halfway down. He lifted the paper sack and dumped the money through the window. As he folded the paper sack it made a crunchy sound. He stuffed the sack inside his zippered jacket. No one was around. The old man's heart seemed to beat erratically. He lay a hand on his chest. Patrolmen inside the building were writing, talking among themselves, and drinking coffee. He saw them through the open windows. He was not noticed. He turned to the highway and strolled casually to it. His heartbeat stabilized. It was easier than he expected. Headlights darted toward him. The patrol car stopped, its luminous insignia on the car door somehow warning him.

"Where are you going, Chief?" the cop at the steering wheel asked.

"Home," the old man replied. "Can you laws give me a lift home? It's just up the road. My heart don't feel so good."

"We don't git paid to haul you around," the orange-haired cop said.

The old man answered, "It's okay. I can git around. Someone'll pick me up, take me home."

As another car approached, the old man put out a shaky hand and the car stopped. He climbed inside. His thoughts were on Sonny. He didn't talk all the way home. In a few minutes, he was standing at his kitchen door.

After her stepfather had gone, Sallie went to old man High Water's house. He was about eighty and was one of the men who had disciplined Sonny earlier. Sallie sat politely at his kitchen table stirring sweet coffee and laughing with High Water and his wife. The laughing stopped. Sallie rose to put a colorful blanket she had brought, wrapped in a towel, on High Water's lap. She sat back down. High Water said nothing. He knew she had come for something.

"Stepdad sent me over. Told me you'd know what to do. It's Sonny," she said.

High Water's wife turned off the kitchen light. The three sat in the thick blue-black dark.

"How bad?" High Water wanted to know.

"Purty bad," Sallie admitted. "That robbery over in town. Sonny's the one."

High Water nodded his head in the dark after she told

her story. She had nothing more to say afterwards. High Water didn't talk either, didn't lay any blame anywhere. He just sat deep in his own thoughts.

"Been a long time," he finally said. "Bout thirty years since the last time."

When Sallie left, High Water's old woman asked, "You going to do it, Earl?"

High Water stood in the dark and said, "If its got to be done. We'll see..." He left it at that, then went out the door into the night to visit other old men who were already in bed.

Sonny staggered into Sallie's house. The windup clock that ticked loudly said it was nearly one. The house was all dark. He pulled the cord beside the door. One light came on.

"Momma," he said, "Your Sonny Boy come home."

When no answer came, he went to Sallie's room. Her bed was empty and still made. He went to his room, sprawled on the army bed. His fingers explored the pillow. Empty.

Sonny howled, ran through the house tearing at things, searching for the lost money. "Who took it?" he screamed. Then he calmed momentarily. "Momma took it," he answered himself. Now he was fighting mad, ugly with rage.

Sallie waited with her old folks. "Daddy," she said to the old man sitting with her in the dark, "I'm scared. Things have gone too far." Her stepfather nodded his head. Sallie's mother reached for Sallie's hand in the dark.

Sonny hit the kitchen door with an iron fist. It went through the glass. "He's here," Sallie's momma said with a slight tremor in her voice.

Sallie went into the kitchen. Sonny was coming through the door. He hit Sallie before she knew it, flung her against the wall and she sagged to the floor.

Sallie forced herself up and said, "Now Sonny, you wrong. It's my fault I guess. I love you so much."

Sonny shoved her against the stove. For some reason, she pictured the old man shoving Sonny some years before.

"Sonny, you got to right it, everything that's wrong," she pleaded.

Sonny turned to Sallie's stepfather who walked in then.

"Where is it?" Sonny yelled at them.

They were silent.

"I said, where is it?" Sonny hollered again.

"Took it back where it belongs," Sallie's stepfather confessed.

"You what?" Sonny shook the old man by the shoulders.

"Leave him alone," Sallie said to Sonny, who slapped her with a hand that sent her reeling again. She bumped into the old man and knocked him against the wall. Sonny hit them both until they slumped on the floor, unable to stand again. He said, "You old folks just don't understand. If we're goin to make it in the whiteman's world, we got to play his games. Learn to play as good as he does. Wise up! He's been stealin from us right along."

He heard a sound behind him. Sonny turned. His grandmother was there, glaring at him. She said, "Boy, you wrong! You whipped your Momma and this poor old man. You left your children and all your women. Now tell me zactly, what's these games you say you playin?"

Sonny's mouth jerked, trying to speak. He stepped threateningly at her.

"Stop it!" she said. "And you hush that big mouth of yours. Or what you planning to do Sonny Boy, whip an old woman? Your body growed big boy, but your brains and heart ain't growed at all!"

Sonny hung his head. He whispered, "I'm sorry, Momma."

Sallie could barely see him. One side of her face and her eyes were slowly turning blue. Her head throbbed.

"It's out of our hands now," Sonny's grandmother said.

"What do you mean?" Sonny asked in a rational tone. "The laws?"

His grandmother was contemptful. "Those white laws can't smoke bunny rabbits out of the hills if they try."

"I ain't scared of white laws anyway," Sonny said. "Ain't scared of anyone. I can whip everyone I know."

His grandmother's eyes lit in the dim lighting. She answered, "No one's ever whipped you Sonny Boy. That's what's wrong."

"Nobody can," Sonny said defiantly, his anger rising again.

He slammed the door loudly as he left, leaving his grandmother to pick up her old man and Sallie.

Sonny had never whipped his folks before. He was uneasy because disturbing memories came back to him. Things he'd forgotten.

The tribe had been known to whip a man when he got too big for his britches, when he acted as if he alone lived in this world. The old men drilled that into Sonny when he was just a little boy. They'd whipped a man a few years before Sonny was born, they said. Whipped him until he was nearly dead. He'd left his children and often whipped his family and old folks too. Sonny cringed and went in search of one more drink.

The next morning Earl High Water knocked on Sallie's folks' door. Sallie opened it. High Water's eyebrows lifted an inch at her appearance. He asked for Sallie's stepfather, and Sallie brought the beat-up old man to him. High Water didn't say a word. He looked at the two of them hard, turned his back, and marched out the door, his eighty-year-old body sinewy and agile.

High Water went directly to another old man. The two talked in low, guarded tones. Then they went through town, out into the hills, to visit with families in teasing tones until the conversation turned more serious. Each host nodded to High Water and his companion as the two departed. The mood of the people was pensive as they remembered something they had witnessed thirty years earlier.

Sonny didn't show himself for several days. Earl High Water went to Sallie in that time and said, "Be this weekend. If he don't show, then next weekend, then the next, til he comes."

Sallie looked down at the floor. "I wish things were different," she said wistfully.

High Water looked at her sharply. He said in a cutting voice, "Now, don't let your heart get in the way this time girl."

She lifted her head to High Water. "No, I won't. It's up to someone else now," she said, fully composed.

Sonny appeared at Liza's place. Liza warned, "Something's going on around here. I don't know what it is, but there's something scary about it."

Sonny laughed at her unexplained fear.

Three weeks later Sonny was his old self again. On weekends he'd been getting sloppy drunk in town, didn't go home. But this weekend ahead, a special event was to be held at the tribal campground.

Sonny spent a lot of time looking at himself as he got ready at Sallie's house. Sallie disappeared from the house now when he was there. When he had told her he was going out to the campground, Sallie kept sewing. She hadn't said much in the last three weeks. As soon as Sonny went to get ready, Sallie left the house.

*"Strange how that money just showed up like that,"* freckled face said.

*"Yeah,"* his partner agreed. *"But he was just glad to get it back, quick like that. It's done with now. He ain't going to press no charges."*

*The police car glided slowly down the street. It was late Saturday morning, the first of two rounds that day.*

*"You don't think that old man we saw the other night had anything to do with it, do you?"* freckled face asked again.

*"That old man?"* the other cop laughed.

*The oranged-haired cop smiled and said, "Naw, I guess not. Didn't look smart enough to pull something like that off."*

It was midday. Sonny stalked the campground. People reclined on blankets and sat on handmade benches. No one appeared to notice him. Sonny had had a drink or two on the way out. "Hey!" he shouted and pounded his chest. "Sonny Boy's here!" The people ignored his shouts. They let him walk to the center of them. Then in one united move, their eyes turned on him. "Too damn good looking," Sonny said to himself and chuckled. The people's faces were unreadable, their eyes clear and cold.

A few hundred people were there, all related to Sonny and each other in complex relationships. Only a few people moved. They were at the center of the crowd and left a circular clearing where two posts stood. Sonny had never seen that before.

Behind him a woman signaled, it was a high pitched

*lau-lau* the women used, made from the tongue hitting the roof of the mouth. Another *lau-lau* answered in front of him. The people had waited for this. They closed in on Sonny.

He started to run, but the people wouldn't let him through. He punched and kicked wildly. They retaliated with violent hits. The women pulled his clothes; the men pinned his arms. The women used wooden clubs and rocks. Sonny hurt—his back, his legs, his arms. The women stoned and beat him until every part of him was sore. The men held him tight, wouldn't let him go. Sonny kicked and struck with all he had but people kept coming at him. His nose bled and his right wrist ached inside. He didn't quit fighting though, striking blindly at anything that moved. He sensed then that the women had moved back, the men were coming in. Sonny was in grueling pain. The men slapped him back and forth. Fists stung his face and broke his teeth. A blow struck him fiercely across his legs. The pain was excruciating and he fell. The men picked Sonny up again and hit him over and over until he tasted salty blood in his mouth. He couldn't stand alone. His legs were hit again. Sonny fell, almost unconscious.

He heard a vaguely familiar voice say, "That's enough. Move him over here."

They dragged Sonny face down through the dirt to the posts. His legs wouldn't hold him but they strung him up tightly by his limp wrists.

High Water held a long rawhide whip. He struck Sonny twice on his back and legs. Then High Water gave the whip to another old man who whipped Sonny once. The whip passed down a long line. The lashings became more fierce as the middle-aged men used the whip.

Sonny had managed to keep from screaming. He didn't want to cry out. But with each crack of the whip, a little more breath was taken from him. He couldn't take any more. He screamed as loud as he could, but surprisingly, it made only a whimpering little sound. His whole body was tender and raw. He surrendered to unconsciousness.

High Water cut him down. Sonny dropped with a heavy, lifeless thud to the ground. The people's eyes glistened; tears streamed down their faces. They began to leave, to make their way to their houses.

Sallie was with her mother and stepfather. They came toward High Water who stood over Sonny. Sallie's eyes were wet. She knelt at Sonny's side.

High Water pulled Sallie's arm, "Don't you touch him!" he said fiercely. "Leave him there and go home. You know how things are."

*At dusk the cops were on patrol. They had decided the campground was unusually deserted for a weekend, not a light or soul in sight. The people all seemed to be hidden. It was unusual. The two cops got out of the patrol car to walk through the campground. The posts were visible, and that seemed irregular, too. They wanted a better look, went up close.*

*A disfigured bloody mess of flesh lay on the ground. "He dead?" the orange-haired man asked.*

*"Close to it," the other one replied.*

*"Who is it?" the orange-haired man asked, as if he really cared.*

*"Can't tell. He sure is beat up good," the other answered, and went back to the patrol car.*

"Man, what happened to you?" the orange-haired cop asked Sonny when he became conscious three days later in the hospital.

Sonny ignored him. He couldn't talk if he tried. His mouth was wired together. His body was on fire. Every part of him hurt. He was bandaged with a cast on his right arm and leg. His very guts hurt.

"You Sonny Hoop?" the other cop asked. Sonny didn't reply.

"Who did this to you?" the same cop questioned for several days. But Sonny's face remained blank. His eyes stayed on the ceiling each day until the cops left.

Sonny was in the hospital nearly three weeks. No one came to visit him. He had a lot of time to think. Revenge was foremost on his mind. He plotted to catch High Water and kill him. Sonny knew that the whole tribe was involved in what had happened to him, but he knew, too, that he couldn't whip and kill the whole tribe. He considered running away, heading up north. The winters were long and cold there.

Sonny lay in bed and scowled during most of his recuperation. Near the end of his stay, he admitted to himself that he dreaded facing any of his people.

Sonny went home to Sallie when he was able, in bandages and casts. His wounds were healing slowly. There were still stitches in his body and face. Sallie didn't embrace him when he returned as she was prone to do after one of his absences. She didn't say very much either. Just pointed to his room. He climbed into bed, tired and aching from his painful journey home.

He was sullen for a long time. He refused to go anywhere. Months passed before he looked any of his people in their eyes, especially his family and children. The wounds were all closed on his body by then, but Sonny pained inside.

*The patrol car was winding down the street. Freckled face was saying, "Got to admit, I'll never in a hunnerd years ever understand what you see in these Indians."*

High Water's old woman said to Earl, "The laws is around again," and pointed to their car.

High Water nodded his head up and down. He said, "Them two laws is funny kind of characters. That orange-haired one don't look smart enough to git around by himself."

High Water's wife cackled in a high-pitched laugh. They stood on their front porch that sagged in the middle. She went inside the house, leaving Earl sitting alone, locusts singing to him.

The bushes in front of the house moved. High Water became motionless.

Sonny stood in the shadows. High Water had been expecting him.

Sonny stepped out slowly, his tortured mind filled with things he'd memorized to say to High Water. High Water's old woman watched Sonny from a window.

"Hey, old man!" Sonny yelled with bravado. "Sonny Boy is here."

Sonny had carefully avoided High Water all these months, and High Water hadn't seen hide nor hair of him.

"So you come back?" High Water asked, unshaken by Sonny's presence.

"That's right," Sonny said. "This boy can't be whipped."

"Uh-huh," High Water said with a windy sigh.

High Water's tone of voice crushed Sonny somehow. Sonny sobbed, great heartbreaking sobs. His massive shadowy figure dropped to its knees.

*The spotlight of the partrol car swept over Sonny, down on his knees before High Water, his face cupped in his huge hands.*

*"What the hell?" freckled face asked his partner.*

*The other cop stopped the car and turned off the lights. They sat there and watched.*

Sonny's tears fell noisily. He had no control. He emptied himself of them, to High Water, then and there. High Water cried with Sonny, too, as did High Water's old woman, hidden behind the door.

When High Water had spent his tears, he asked Sonny in a husky voice, "Sonny Boy, what you crying for?"

Sonny laughed and cried at once, "I don't really know, except that it's been too long since I've cried and been a boy. What are *you* crying for?"

"It's one of the laws, boy," High Water told him. "We can't let none of our people cry alone."

High Water went and picked Sonny off the ground. He embraced him tightly before they went into the house.

*"I'll be damned," said the orange-haired cop to the other. "What in hell just went on?"*

*The driver turned the spotlight on High Water's place. Everything was as it should have been there, not an unexplained shadow anywhere. The car purred as the two cops drove off.*

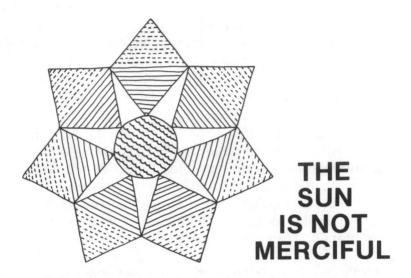

# THE
# SUN
# IS NOT
# MERCIFUL

*A*s far as the eye can see, the lake is still, is dark at its edges, but patches shimmer blue and gold, dip and swirl into myriads of other colors at the center of the lake. The sun is beating down on the luminous water, beating down on the dried brown grass and the trees plagued with worms and other infestations. Lydia is sitting at the water's edge, a cane fishing pole in her right hand. Her skirt billows over the boulder. Her forehead is dripping sweat, which she wipes away in one stroke with her other sun-baked brown arm. She can feel the sweat slipping under her dress. It's rolling in cool drops between her breasts, down her back, and stops at her waist where her dress is damp. But Lydia doesn't move. Her eyes stay on the red and white cork sitting on the water.

Voices float to Lydia from across the lake, and the motor boats drown the vague words and hint of laughter in their choppy, splashing, whirring sounds. Lydia ignores the contraptions laying on the lake, the water skiers walking on the water, the șails aimlessly adrift.

Impatiently, she waves them away, the sights and sounds the place is now. Her dimming sight takes in the knoll on the east rim of the lake. She doesn't see it well, but feels it there. The trees she knows to be there, tough eerie-shaped cedar trees, do not yield to the sun that is whipping all life down without mercy.

Bertha is coming down the hill on the path behind Lydia. Bertha is younger than Lydia by a year. Bertha's ample body shakes with each step, and her gray hair, parted in the middle of her head, clings to her round face above the braids that swing just above her wide hips.

Bertha calls to Lydia, "The sun is not merciful. Remember Old Man always said, 'The sun is not merciful' "?

Lydia can hear Bertha panting. It's the water slapping the shore. Again the voices and laughter drift over the lake, the deep, still water, and linger in the lap of Lydia's calf-length skirt. But her eyes remain stuck on the red plastic ball protruding from the water.

Bertha touches Lydia's white hair, which hangs in loose unkempt waves to Lydia's shoulders. The thick white mass is wet at the scalp. Bertha pins up Lydia's hair in two sections, one above each of Lydia's ears. Glass beads in a red, white, and blue chevron glitter from the pins above Lydia's ears when Lydia moves. The glistening on Lydia's hair makes Bertha's eyes squint, as does the sun laying in the water and the sky.

Bertha sits on the boulder beside Lydia. She says, "Hope there's no snakes under this rock. That's all we need, a snake coming out at us."

Lydia's head glistens at Bertha, and Lydia says, "Too damn hot for snakes." Lydia takes the bundle Bertha has carried down the path. Lydia slowly unfolds the scarf that holds the contents together. There are hanks of turquoise, gold, and black glass beads in the creases of the flowered black headscarf. Each one sparkles at Bertha and Lydia.

There is also a piece of yellow wax, thread, and long thin beading needles with a pair of scissors, one of the blades broken in half.

Bertha searches the pocket of her housedress for a medallion she is creating, beading. It is more than halfway done. Her fingers run over the smooth rippling surface of her handiwork. She selects the gold beads she needs and waxes her thread. Little drops of water roll down her temples and cling there.

The pole in Lydia's hand yanks; the cork pops under the water and reappears. Lydia waits patiently for it to go under again, ignoring the voracious laughter on the lake's opposite shore. The cork is sucked under again and doesn't appear for a few seconds. Lydia lifts her cane pole and pulls in her catch. It is silvery, the same silver as the lake. It glistens, and its tail fin swishes back and forth, spraying drops of water on Lydia's sun-creased face.

A jeep is coming down the dirt road, the dust rising behind it, a dead giveaway of its speeding approach.

Bertha has seen it with her sharp eyes, but she has waited to be certain before she says, "Ranger's coming sure as shooting." That's all she says and goes back to her beading.

Lydia's mouth sets in a crooked line. She baits her hook again with an earthworm the color of slick mud, and the worm wriggles. Lydia throws in her line. And waits.

The jeep stops at the end of the road on the other side of the barbed-wire fence, about half a mile from Lydia and Bertha. The dust following the jeep settles. The sun beats it down.

"What's he doing down yonder?" Lydia asks, her weak eyes barely defining a red sail in the middle of the water. She looks back over her shoulder to the dirt road where the jeep has stopped. Her hair pins glisten.

"He's heading this way," Bertha answers. A figure is

moving toward them, a spot that grows as it draws in on them.

"Ah reckon there's going to be trouble sometime," Lydia says, squinting at the figure now taking shape.

When he gets to Lydia and Bertha, he is panting hard and his breath is hot. He is wearing a hat with a brim and his uniform is several shades darker around the neck and under the arms. He is carrying a tablet in one hand. His eyes are the same color as his hat. His face is bright red.

"The sun is not merciful," Lydia says to him, as he watches the red cork. Bertha picks up a few more gold beads, then squints up at the man. "That you, Hollis?" Bertha says. "Glad it be you. Don't want any trouble."

"Now ladies," he says to them, "you know you're not supposed to be out here. You're trespassing again. How many times you have to be told? We're going to have to do something about this situation, something effective. Going to have to fine you."

Lydia says, "How much is the fine, Hollis?" She feels the sweat dripping down her back as she speaks.

"More'n you two got," Hollis says. "Damn near five hunnerd dollars."

"You right Hollis, we don't have five hunnerd dollars. Guess you going to have to haul us off," Lydia says. Her red cork is moving in spirals on the glassy water.

Hollis lifts off his hat. His yellow hair is all squashed into his head marking the hatband line. His amber eyes go to the sails on the lake, the motor boats stirring the deep water.

"Set yourself down, Hollis," Lydia says to him. "Cool down a bit. The sun is not merciful. It beats on everything, all alike."

Hollis is sitting down, on a boulder just beside Bertha. He is dipping a hand into the lake, splashing water onto his neck and back.

"How many you catch?" he asks Lydia.

"Eight," Lydia admits.

"Got a license yet?" he asks.

"Nope," Lydia says.

"Never seen women fishing alone before, before you two." Hollis says. One of his hands is submerged in the water. His hair is drying and his face is turning its natural pink.

"No?" Lydia says. She looks at Bertha and says, "No? Heck, Hollis, we been fishing since time began. Can't stop now."

A motor boat is whirring at the three people sitting at the water's edge. Its motor stops not far from them. The shiny black boat halts. Lydia can make out four people in it, two women and two men. They are scantily dressed. One woman's hair is the color of Bertha's flour sack that holds rice on the kitchen wall, though the woman appears to be quite young. Her voice sounds youthful too, high and giddy. Lydia frowns at the intruders. Bertha keeps tacking gold beads.

Hollis looks thoughtfully from the motor boat to Lydia and to Bertha. Children laugh and shriek on the other side of the lake.

Hollis is staring at the power plant and dam on the farthest shore. They sit on the hazy, humid horizon.

Hollis says, "They'll be some new summer homes going up soon now, next month or so, over on the east shore." Lydia's face is impassive. Bertha's face is impassive.

When the two women do not respond to his conversation, Hollis stands and says, "Look ladies, this is going to be my last warning. Next time, it may not be me who has to come out here. Next person might be hard on you. If you want to fish, get a license. See here, I'll even buy one for you Miss Lydia, ma'am, if you would permit me. Ain't cost much. Then you have to fish only in those places designated for fishing. Understand? I been through this with you before."

Lydia is saying, "You want these fish ah caught Hollis? By law, you entitled to them." She looks up at him, now watching his face to see how he will respond.

His face wrinkles and he says, "No, ma'am. You caught them. I don't want them."

Lydia says, "Well, Hollis, you keep throwing fish up to me. Be sure now that you don't want to count or eat them. Ah offered."

Hollis is shaking his head no. He is standing over Lydia, blocking out the unmerciful sun. He says to Lydia, "Promise me now that you all won't come fishing here no more if I let you off today. Promise me that you going to go right down and get a license and fish over yonder with everybody else. Promise me?" His voice carries over the water.

Lydia is looking up at Hollis. She is saying, "How many times we talked now Hollis? Five times? Six?" Hollis nods.

Lydia is saying, "Ah told you each time, ah can't do what you're asking. If ah could, ah would. Can't help it, Hollis."

He had erected the house down in the valley between the corn and alfalfa and rows of cotton. Old Man himself nailed the whole thing together, dug out the deep cellar to store pungent herbs and other plants, put up the outhouse—a "two-seater"—and a two-story barn and tool shed. Old Man turned the ground in the dewy springtime to keep the corn growing, picked cockleburs from the long rows of cotton bolls, slopped the snorting pigs, fed the continually pecking, clucking chickens, as well as the cows that stared at Lydia and Bertha with unblinking eyes as they chewed cud and swiped horseflies with their frayed tails, and the big work horses that slowly pulled the wagon and the plow through the fields. Lydia hadn't been there when he put up the house, but she took part in everything else. The house was raised about 1910, nearly seventy years ago, and that's how Lydia knew that her own seventieth birthday was approaching in the fall.

Old Man taught the little girls to fish as soon as they could toddle to the creeks winding around the corn and through the cotton and alfalfa fields.

Old Man said to them when they were very young, "Girls, my mother used to bind my cradleboard to the trees and run a fishing line from my board to the creeks and ponds. Ah brought in some whoppers fore ah ever learned to crawl."

Fishing was good year round, and Bertha and Lydia trailed after Old Man through winter and summer with a fishing pole over their shoulders and bait in their other hands.

Winter fishing was bearable. The girls could hide from the cold in Old Man's big old echoing house, and the womenfolk always dressed the girls bulky and warm. But summer fishing came harder, was something the two girls had to learn to tolerate. The wet heat on the creek banks was intensely heavy and stifling, getting into the girls' eyes and suffocating them in a damp blanket. The heat was a presence or burning force they could not escape or outrun, though they tried to hide from it by laying spread eagle on the cooler ground between the rows of green corn stalks. The corn stalks offered shade, but the heat seeped into the cornfield maze as they fingered cornsilk and worms off the green corn. They struggled against the searing rays of the sun, futilely attempting to cast it off their sunburned arms cooked to a red-brown.

Old Man told them, "Don't fight the sun, girls. Let it be. It's going to whip you down if you fight it. Let it be."

Eventually they learned to respect the power of it,

accepted the wavy lines of heat that rose from the ground into the air, the cool mirages beyond the corn and alfalfa fields. Old Man taught the girls how to deal with the heat; how to sit perfectly still, like the dragonflies that poised themselves on the girls' fishing poles; how to breathe and suck in the precious air they needed to survive on the oppressively humid creekbanks; how to shade themselves when they felt they might faint from it; and how to judge the wind to catch rare breezes sifting through the thick grove of trees. And Bertha and Lydia learned. They caught hundreds of fish, and turtles too. Soon the unmerciful sun was not so bad. Bertha and Lydia could tolerate midday, could hang over the edge of the ponds and creeks like fragile, delicate dragonflies poised in one posture indefinitely, while their bodies were heavy, bathed in weighty perspiration—droplets of it running in curvy lines into the corners of their eyes and hanging from the tips of their noses, chins, and jawlines until the drops finally released themselves without sound into the creeks and ponds surrounding Old Man's house.

Old Man said, "Girls, we're fishermen from way back yonder, way back when time first began. Fact is, alla us came outta water. Happened up north, round Canada somewhere. Well, girls, we found ourselves on the shore of this wide lake. We came outta it, see? Weren't no other people then—just us back then. And that's why we're fishermen from way back, fore time even began."

"How'd we get here?" Lydia asked Old Man when she was going on seven years. Bertha and she waited for Old Man's reply as they washed pearly white shells in the warm creek water.

"We walked," Old Man said. "Damn near walked all over this old earth: First we walked from way up north, wandered around a bit for a few years, trying to get our bearings ah guess. Then we began to drift southward. Groups of people got tired of wandering around all the time, so they began to drop off, break away and settle down. But us, we weren't tired. We kept on the move, following rivers and creekbeds til we finally stopped along a river in Nebraska. Know where that is? It's up north, bout a four-week walk from here. Anyway, we stayed in Nebraska another hundred years and more. Then some strangers came, came close enough to walk through the midst of us. To make a long story short, we up and left Nebraska not long after that. Came down here on foot with our food and clothing carried on covered wagons and pack animals. Ah remember that, ah made the trip myself. Was a little feller near your age. Yes, sir, recollect that. We walked for nearly four weeks to get down here."

Old Man lay back, perfectly still on the narrow creekbank. His eyes studied the tree tops overhead. Bertha and Lydia laid their shells aside when Old Man lay down. They walked to him, their bare footprints stayed deep in the mud. They stood over him for a moment. His face and arms were the color of squishy red sand on the creekbanks. His eyes shone like the rocks and pebbles in the water winking at them. His face glistened in places from sweat and oil on his forehead and temples.

Lydia became more aware of the creek in the silence, the shadows in the thick green trees and brush, the dark spots on the other bank. Lydia asked, "Are you all right Old Man?"

Old Man's eyes went from the tree tops to Lydia's face. The whites of his eyes were the same texture and color as the shells she had cleaned.

"Ah'm all right," he smiled. "My thoughts are just on other things right now."

Lydia and Bertha lay down on each side of Old Man. Lydia put her arms under her head. The three watched the trees above them. Redbirds flitted from limb to limb, brilliant streaks of color that lit the afternoon for Lydia and Bertha like no other day to come for many a year.

That was a particularly steamy day, and the girls wiped the hot spray from their eyes. Old Man told them to sit in the water when he noticed the beads of sweat around their necks, the sweat pouring down their temples. They took off their worn dresses, caked with sand from laying beside Old Man on the creekbank. Wearing only their underwear, they sat waist deep in the brown water until Old Man finally led the way home.

When Lydia was twenty-two, Old Man and Lydia's mother gave Lydia away to another family who had asked for Lydia, for their son. The marriage was arranged and Lydia lived with them for fifteen years. In that time, Lydia had three sons. Bertha's marriage was arranged not too long after Lydia's, and she stayed married until her husband died four years later. By then Bertha had had a sickly child.

Old Man died in '58. Old Man's fisherpeople dug him a deep grave on the knoll east of the house and planted Old Man up there. Lydia and her family took over Old Man's house after that. Later, Bertha with her thin but pretty daughter, returned to Old Man's house too.

Lydia was old now. Old Man had fathered her when he was in his fifties; Bertha, too.

They are carrying Lydia to the car that is held together with wires. The passenger windows are all broken. The front windshield is cracked, leaving an impression of veins through which the road is viewed.

The men have made a seat between them with their brown arms. Lydia is seated there, riding on the human net with her arms thrown over each of the two men's shoulders. Lydia's one leg dangles in the air. She is wearing a tennis shoe on her one foot. The men step carefully toward the car, taking slow steps so that they will not drop Lydia. Lydia's eyes are on the ground watching it move under her. Bertha is following several paces behind Lydia and the men. She is carrying a stringer of fish that gleam in the afternoon sun.

The lake behind Bertha shimmers, rippling toward Bertha and then away from her. Bertha watches the men lift Lydia into the back seat of the car. Lydia's hairpins are glossy in the shade of the car. The men have carried Lydia over a hundred feet.

Bertha stops where she is as soon as Lydia is safely in the beat-up car. Lydia is fanning herself with a faded magazine, the pages dry and brown. Bertha shades her forehead with a hand and turns east to the knoll on that shore. From the back seat of the car, Lydia, too, tries to focus on the knoll, but it remains fuzzy, more felt than seen.

The two men wait, leaning against the shady side of the car. The roof of the car is hot and shiny behind them. The men watch the boats dart back and forth over the water.

Bertha is moving toward the car, her ample body shaking softly with each step. She is saying something, but her words are not distinguishable while the yelling of swimmers on the opposite shore is clearly heard by Lydia and the two men.

Bertha climbs into the back seat of the car beside Lydia. One of the men slams Bertha's door. The man who is driving turns the key in the car. For a minute, it threatens not to start, but then it chokes and the whining engine can be heard on the opposite shore.

The driver steers carefully in the direction of the barbed-wire fence to the narrow opening where the car has been forced through. Bertha is watching the landscape as the car crawls to the road. She notes the height of the sunflowers, the plants used as herbs and medicines. Lydia is observing the same.

When the car finally reaches the fence, Lydia asks the driver, "Are you going to take us home son?" His eyes find hers in the rearview mirror, and he says, "Wherever you want to go, Momma."

Lydia is looking back over her shoulder. She is saying, "Ah want to go home son."

His eyes meet hers again in the mirror and he nods.

Lydia and Bertha sat in the shade beside the creek that ran below the house south of the cornfield that day, three years ago. It was September and the creek had gone dry, the fish and turtles disappeared, too. There had been no rain for 100 days in a row. Clouds occasionally drifted over Lydia and Bertha, but the rainless summer went unbroken into the fall. The water level of the half-dozen ponds in the area had dipped dangerously low; the livestock grazing in the burned pastures beyond the houses had water trucked to them every other day now. It was on that day that a car crossed the creek south of the house, crossed the dry creekbed crusted into thousands of jigsaw pieces stretching east and west into the trees. Lydia and Bertha saw the car brake at the house 300 yards away from them, saw four people step out of the sedan. The house was empty. The visitors stood at the crooked screen door for a minute and looked around the house. Bertha waved, and the visitors approached.

The faces of the visitors were grim. There were three men and a woman. Bertha offered them a drink of water which they accepted, drinking the warm water from the same white enamel cup.

"What brings you out so far on a day like this?" Lydia asked, waving a woven Japanese fan over her face.

"Brung some bad news to you folks today," the woman said as the men let her speak.

Lydia's fan waved a mite slower, and Bertha looked at the woman curiously. "Get on with it," Lydia said.

The woman paused briefly before the words came. "You haven't come to the Council meetings these last few weeks. Ah reckon your leg is still bothering you?" The woman looked at Lydia's leg, swollen to twice its size below the knee.

Lydia replied, "They gonna take it off. Soon ah suppose. It was bound to happen if it didn't get any better." Lydia's face was impassive as if she were talking about someone else.

The woman cleared her throat and turned to one of the men. She said to him, "Jake, you tell em."

Jake looked at his two men companions and nodded his head. Jake said, "Lydia, we brung some bad news. You heard the talk these past few months about the state wanting to buy up all our land, tribal land, the old folks' allotments?"

He waited a minute to let his question sink into Bertha and Lydia. A single cloud moved over the group, casting an imperfect circle on the ground.

Bertha responded, "The sun is not merciful. No rain for how many days?"

Lydia looked at her leg. Lydia said, "They gonna have to take off the leg any day now. It's gonna have to go..."

Jake said, "Lydia, this property is in your name. They paying good money for the land. Some of us already sold, but then they's a few of us who don't want to go, don't want to leave this place. We're gonna hold out for as long as we can."

Lydia massaged her purple leg, and Bertha frowned at the cracking ground.

Another man came forward and took some papers out of his back pants pocket. He handed it to Lydia and said, "Lydia, your property comes to nearly fifteen thousand dollars. They'll go even higher I'm sure. Get one of your boys to go over these here papers with you."

Lydia stared at the papers in her hand, not reading or seeing them. Bertha watched Lydia carefully, and then Bertha asked, "What they want it for, Jake? What they want the land for?"

"They gonna flood it, Bertha. Build a big recreation area and power plant purty close to where my house stands at this very time. All this place, your place, Lydia, is gonna be under water. Hate to see it," Jake said. "Hate to see it."

"Did you sell out?" Lydia asked Jake in an unemotional voice.

"Nawh, nawh, Lydia. Gonna fight it best ah can. Us four here are the only ones so far who ain't sold yet. But money's strong, Lydia. Don't know how long we gonna hold out. We'll do the best we can. You with us, Lydia, or agin us? Want to talk it over with the kids first?" He looked from Lydia to Bertha.

Lydia responded. "Don't need to talk to nobody, Jake." Lydia fanned herself frantically, but her voice was calm. She added, "Old Man's place not for sale. Old Man's place not for sale, not for alla money in the world."

Bertha, who had been sitting frowning at the ground, lifted her head. She wore a broad smile. She went over to Lydia and hugged her, then turned to her visitors and said, "You heard Lydia. Old Man's place is not up for grabs."

The visitors nodded to each other visibly relieved. Their grim faces were softer.

The six people sat under the trees for awhile, not speaking but fanning themselves with Lydia's papers they had brought to her. Finally, Bertha asked, "How we gonna do it? How you fight something like this?"

Jake answered, "Don't rightly know, Bertha. Don't really know if you can fight it. Those people down south, I forget what tribe they are, they couldn't fight it even though they tried like crazy. Been studying up on this.

Drove up to town the other day and visited the libary. This kind of thing is happening all over, to tribes all over this whole United States. Ain't nobody ever won."

The group was quiet again. Their faces became pinched and tight. Finally Jake rose and led the visitors to their car.

The drought broke in early October with a spray of soft, hot rain. Lydia and Bertha sat outside in it, their grandchildren played beside them in the mud. The rain fell lightly on them, but pressure on Lydia's bad leg was intense. It had turned a sick shade of gray. Bertha loaded Lydia into the old beat-up car. Bertha herself drove Lydia to the hospital where she left Lydia alone the next day.

When Bertha and Lydia's sons came to take Lydia home four weeks later, Lydia was wheeled out to the parking lot so the men could lift her into the car. Only one leg dangled beneath her body. She wore a black shoe with a thick high heel. The men tied the wheelchair to the trunk of the car with a piece of rope.

The ride home took an hour and a half. The plains had turned gray in her absence, though the weather was mild yet. The houses along the way had been abandoned. Livestock that usually grazed in the pastures were gone, too. New fences were thrown up, and signs were posted every half mile or so. The signs said NO TRESPASSING in big bright letters. Beneath one of the signs, a quarter of a mile from Lydia's house, Lydia ordered her son to stop the car. He turned off the key and turned to his mother. Lydia said, "Help me out son. I want to go outside."

He took the wheelchair from the back of the car and unfolded it. Then he lifted his mother and set her in the chair. Lydia turned to Bertha and said, "Bertha, come here." Bertha got out of the car and went to Lydia. Lydia said, "Let's walk, Sister. Push me." Then Lydia turned to the men standing around the car. To them Lydia said, "Go on home boys, we gonna walk from here."

One of the men looked at his mother sitting there in the shiny new wheelchair, the newly erected fence rising behind her with a NO TRESPASSING sign challenging anyone to go beyond it into forbidden territory. Lydia wore a black headscarf with red and pink roses on it, tied under her chin. Slips of hair fell out of the headscarf, and the wind tossed the strands across her face.

The other man looked back down the road they had just traveled to Lydia's and Bertha's house in the distance, and to the miles of new fence and signs that Lydia hadn't seen before. The sky was starting to darken in the north, a storm was on the way. The man said, "Momma, you sure that chair is gonna make it to the house?" His eyes went from Lydia to Bertha, two old figures beside the road.

Lydia nodded, "We be all right, son. You boys go on home."

Lydia's son turned to Bertha and said, "Aunt Bertha, if there's some reason you can't push her home, we'll come and get you."

Bertha nodded, her arms hung limply at her side. She pushed Lydia toward the fence as the car started down the road. Lydia's hands explored the barbed-wire fence and it pricked her finger. Lydia sucked the dark blood from the cut on her hand and said to Bertha, "How many of us left, Bertha? Looks like everybody but you and me is gone."

Bertha nodded. She sat down on the ground beside Lydia's wheelchair and looked up into Lydia's eyes. Bertha said sadly, "You know Lydia, we're fighting a losing battle. We not gonna win."

Lydia reached over and pulled one of Bertha's braids. Lydia said, "Bertha, member the time Old Man taught us to swim?" Her scarf billowed around her face with a growing wind.

Bertha grinned and said, "For fisherpeople, it took us

a hell of a long time just to learn to float. Who would ever guess that we of all people had ever come out of the water way back yonder when time began? Ah was as heavy as a rock, kept sinking to the bottom. Old Man kept pulling me up just before my lungs completely filled with water." Bertha was laughing.

Lydia turned toward the direction of the pond where she and Bertha learned to swim. The pond lay hidden two miles behind the new fence. Bertha got up and began to push Lydia down the road, the gray sky in the north was rolling south and east.

Lydia looked eastward from the sky to the knoll where eerie-shaped cedar trees clung tightly to the rocks and boulders covering the hill. Bertha looked up there too and silently pushed Lydia toward the house.

"Ah miss my leg, Bertha," Lydia said. "Ah miss my ankle and my toes and my toenails, too. Sometimes it feels like it's still there, but ah look at it and ah don't see it and ah know that it must not be there. Ah'm gonna miss it bad, Bertha. Don't seem right somehow to go through life having to throw away one shoe each time you buy a new pair."

"Ah know," Bertha said.

The road was bumpy. Lydia bounced up and down. Bertha guided the wheelchair firmly down the road.

"How much time we got?" Lydia asked Bertha. Lydia tried to angle her face and body toward Bertha, behind her. "How much time we got here? People done left most of the land around us."

Bertha answered in a question, "Six months?"

"That's what ah figger," Lydia said. "Come spring, we in for trouble."

The strange men came inside Lydia's house in May. There were eight of them, and there was Bertha and Lydia. The men wore business suits, permapress slacks, and pale pastel shirts. One of the men pressed a check in Lydia's hand. He said, "Better take it, Miss Lydia. If you don't, the land is going to be condemned anyway and you'll be paid less. Then you'll have to accept whatever is given you. Better take that check now. We been patient. We've tried to be patient men. Ten days from now you must be off the land." The men left Lydia's house. The screen door slammed hard.

Bertha took the check from Lydia's hand. It was made out in an amount of more than fourteen thousand dollars. Bertha and Lydia then sat in Old Man's house quietly the rest of the day. Toward evening, Bertha began to weep silently. Big tears rolled down her face and hung on her chin before they slipped loose. Lydia didn't shed tears but made snuffling sounds most of that day and night.

The following morning, Lydia and Bertha began to pack household items. Toward noon, Lydia's sons returned to Lydia's house and Lydia and Bertha told them the bad news.

"Where will you go?" one of the men asked. "Where do you want to go, Momma? Aunt Bertha?"

Bertha replied, "We'll go to that old log cabin on the back road to town. It was our grandfather's place when the people first moved down from Nebraska. No one's used it for years. We'll have to carry water to it, until we can settle somewheres else. You know that cabin ah mean? It's gonna need work, but nothing we can't handle. It won't be going underwater, if those people stick to their plan. And ah think we still have claim to it."

Nine days later, the men carried Lydia out of that house for the last time, to the car where she sat without a word on the long, slow drive out. Her and Bertha's possessions had already been transported and relocated. At first, Lydia's face stuck out of the car window, her hands tightly clutched the door. As the house disappeared from behind them, Lydia inched herself back into the seat, until she was a small bundle in the corner of the car. Bertha was not quiet; she talked all the way. She did not allow herself time to breathe properly. Her words caught on her short breaths and her eyes were brightly glazed. She said, "Old Man was a fisherman from way back," in a fast string of words. "Lydia and ah washed shells down there." Bertha looked toward the creek. "The shells were the color of the white in Old Man's eyes." On and on Bertha talked, until the car stopped at the old log cabin. By then, Bertha was exhausted, her face frightfully pale.

The men pulled Bertha out of the car, talking to her gently. "Aunt Bertha, you were right. This log cabin is gonna be just what you need." The men led her to a makeshift bed covered with sheets and blankets her grandchildren had already made. One of the men said to her, "Aunt Bertha, why don't you just lay down for awhile." Bertha nodded and slumped on the bed.

Then the two men lifted Lydia from the car to the house and set her down on an army cot. Lydia said, "Boys, ah'm kinda tired. Think ah'll just sleep for awhile."

One of the men answered, "Sure, Momma. Get a little rest for yourself. We'll look after things while you sleep." The men went out the door.

Outside, one of the men lit a cigarette and inhaled deeply before turning to search his brother's face. The other man was watching him. They didn't say anything to one another. One of them walked to the car and hit his fist on a sagging door. "Damn!" he said. The other man watched his brother pound the car as he continued to puff on his cigarette. Smoke rose around him.

It came from behind the knoll near Lydia's now destroyed house. Smoke billowed up behind the knoll in a windy gust. Bertha called Lydia from the other side of the cabin. Lydia wheeled herself to where Bertha was. Bertha said, "Look over yonder. Looks like fire over there." They were a long way from the fire, but the smoke could be seen lifting off the hazy plains.

"That's Jake's place," Lydia said thoughtfully.

"Ah know," Bertha said, scrunching her eyebrows together.

At the burning place, Jake stood before his house and barn, set afire by a crew of strange men. Jake was alone with the men, and he wept loudly without shame. He'd still had a few possessions remaining in his three-room house.

Lydia sat in her wheelchair, her shoulders slumped. She said hoarsely to Bertha, "Ah guess Jake meant it when he said they'd have to burn him out."

The men carry Lydia from the car. She is wearing a printed black and gold dress of cotton. The black part of the print is faded in spots, and the material is gauze-thin at the elbows, the bosom, and seat of the dress. Her one foot swings under her, wearing a white tennis shoe. Her shoelace connects only the top eyelets of the shoe. It is a memorable morning in July. The sun is one-third of the way across the flat blue color of the sky. The horizon is hazy, the power plant rises in the north. The lake is gray-green, speaking in splashy, lapping sounds. It is already hot. The ground and the lake are warm.

The men set Lydia on a boulder, just above the deep drop into the still water. Trees shade her on each side. Bertha comes down the path to Lydia. She is carrying a cane fishing pole, a can of bait, a paper sack with lunch, and a bundle of beads. Her body bounces softly like the gentle waves. The men meet Bertha on their way back to the car.

"Aunt Bertha," one of them says, "we'll be back toward sundown."

Bertha says, "Take your time boys. We not going anywhere."

In a few minutes the old car leaves a trail of dust down the road.

"It's going to be a scorcher today," Bertha says to Lydia as Lydia baits her hook.

"Yep," Lydia says.

They sit there all day listening to the people on the opposite shore. The boats slice through the deep water.

A little past noon Lydia says, "It would be easy to roll over, off this drop, into the water down there. The water's got to be twenty feet deep there. Remember when we used to pick mushrooms under here?"

Bertha holds her beading needle up in the air. Her face looks surprised. She scolds Lydia. "You surprise me, Lydia, talking that way. Don't even think it."

"Oh, don't worry, Bertha, ah won't do it, though ah can't say that ah haven't thought of it," Lydia says. "Ah don't feel sorry for myself, really. It's just the world isn't made for one-legged people. Ah'm without a part of me, even though sometimes ah sense that it's still there."

A fish and game motor boat works its way down the shoreline to Bertha and Lydia. They act as if they are unaware of it. In a few minutes, the boat is beside them. Someone waves from the boat. Lydia and Bertha do not respond. Then the boat whirs away again.

The sun is now upon Lydia and Bertha. The trees offer little shade. Shadows are small.

Lydia has a line in the water when Hollis' jeep comes tearing down the road. "Comes Hollis," Bertha tells Lydia softly. Bertha wipes her face free of sweat.

He is strutting down the road, angrily moving toward them. When he arrives, his face and arms are sweaty. He is angry and indignant. He does not greet Bertha and

Lydia but begins to spit words at them. He says, "Now ladies, this time I'm going to fine you. Going to put an end to this nonsense."

Lydia and Bertha do not react to him. Both attempt to cover themselves from the sun in whatever way they can manage. Hollis writes angrily on his tablet. "What's your full name Miss Lydia?" he asks.

Lydia says, "Lydia Mae Wind."

He writes that down, pressing his pencil hard on the tablet.

"Address?" he asks, as Lydia looks up at the trees to find the best shade.

"Route 2," Lydia says. "You welcome to visit us Hollis, whenever you can."

"Age?" he asks. Lydia answers, "Be seventy in the fall."

"That's sixty-nine," he says. "Say sixty-nine then." He is writing again.

"Sixty-nine then," Lydia answers. Lydia leans over the edge of the boulder she is sitting on. Dragonflies hang on her fishing pole and line.

When Hollis is through interrogating Lydia, Bertha puts her needle down and says, "Now it's my turn. My name is Bertha Old Soldier. Ah'm sixty-seven, be sixty-eight in a few months. Ah was born here," she said, "beneath this old lake, this reck-re-ashun area. What else you wanna know?" She is looking up at Hollis in a frown. Her braids rest in her lap, beneath the scarf with beads. The sun shines directly into her glistening face.

Hollis tears a piece of paper from the tablet and hands it to Lydia. Lydia accepts the paper and stuffs it into her dress pocket without looking at it. As she pushes the paper into the pocket, she shifts her body and her one leg with the tennis shoe becomes obvious. Then she lifts her body with her arms and pulls herself under the shade to her left. It is just a spot of shade, but she is out of the sun.

Hollis stares at her one leg. He is quiet for a minute or more. Lydia and Bertha both lift their faces to see him. They see him staring at Lydia's leg. His face turns a bright red, and he lifts his eyes to the sails in the middle of the lake. The lake shimmers, winks at him.

Lydia says to him, "Set yourself down a minute Hollis."

He drops at Lydia's side. He gulps and says, "You know Miss Lydia, I never noticed before that there's a part of you that's missing."

Lydia smiles and answers, "Over two years now. Since this lake's been here."

"How do you get around?" Hollis asks, pulling off his hat and brushing out his mashed-down hair with his fingers.

Bertha laughs and says, "Lydia gets around pretty good. Maybe better than we do."

"Who brings you here?" Hollis asks, his eyes on the power plant on the other side of the lake.

Lydia answers, "My sons."

"Why?" Hollis asks again in disbelief. "An old woman like you?"

Lydia smiles and says, "Because I *want* them to bring me out here."

"Don't they care about you?" Hollis asks. "You shouldn't be out here alone—just you two. It's so hot. You have just one leg. My God!"

Bertha looks at Hollis. She says, "Hollis, this is exactly where ah'm supposed to be. No doubt about that."

Lydia stretches her leg. She asks Hollis, "How old are you Hollis? You from around here?"

Hollis shakes his head no and says, "No, ma'am. I'm

from up in Missouri and I'm twenty-eight. Been down here for about three years now."

Bertha smiles at Hollis. She says, "We were there, once, long time ago, right after time began when we were wandering around a lot then."

Hollis looks puzzled, and he asks, "What keeps bringing you two ladies out here anyway?"

Lydia sits perfectly still. Sweat dots her creased forehead. Only her lips move. She says, "There's a hill over yonder on the east shore, Hollis. Can you see it? Ah can't see that far anymore, but ah feel it sitting there."

Hollis looks at the knoll with the cedar trees.

Lydia says, "That's what's calling us here, Hollis. See this lake, the deep water. That's what calls us here. We fisherpeople, Hollis. Fished since time began. We came up outta water, Hollis, water that looked pretty much like this here. My heart is in the water, Hollis. Can't be drowned, Hollis. We bound to keep coming back, Hollis. Have to, there's no other way."

Hollis stares at Lydia's shoelace. He says, "I'll take that paper back, Miss Lydia."

Lydia looks at him and says, "Nothing says you got to take it back, Hollis."

He says, "No, Miss Lydia, I'll take it."

Lydia digs into her pocket, pulling out the paper. She hands it to him. As he takes the paper, Bertha says, "It's a scorcher today, Hollis." He pulls on his hat and begins to walk away from them.

Bertha starts beading again. She lifts her head to Lydia and says, "Nice kid. He thinks he understands."

Lydia nods, "Yep, ah know. But he don't really understand at all."

"Ah know," Bertha agrees.

The two women hang over the edge of the lake, like delicate poised dragonflies, waiting for the sun to cool, waiting for sundown to come. Lydia's voice travels to the opposite shore, sounding like it is lifting from the deep, still water. She says, "The sun is not merciful, Bertha, not at all."

## Other titles from Firebrand Books include:

*Artemis In Echo Park,* Poetry by Eloise Klein Healy/$8.95

*Beneath My Heart,* Poetry by Janice Gould/$8.95

*The Big Mama Stories* by Shay Youngblood/$8.95

*A Burst Of Light,* Essays by Audre Lorde/$7.95

*Cecile,* Stories by Ruthann Robson/$8.95

*Crime Against Nature,* Poetry by Minnie Bruce Pratt/$8.95

*Diamonds Are A Dyke's Best Friend* by Yvonne Zipter/$9.95

*Dykes To Watch Out For,* Cartoons by Alison Bechdel/$6.95

*Dykes To Watch Out For: The Sequel,* Cartoons by Alison Bechdel /$8.95

*Exile In The Promised Land,* A Memoir by Marcia Freedman/$8.95

*Eye Of A Hurricane,* Stories by Ruthann Robson/$8.95

*The Fires Of Bride,* A Novel by Ellen Galford/$8.95

*Food & Spirits,* Stories by Beth Brant (*Degonwadonti*)/$8.95

*Free Ride,* A Novel by Marilyn Gayle/$9.95

*A Gathering Of Spirit,* A Collection by North American Indian Women edited by Beth Brant (*Degonwadonti*)/$10.95

*Getting Home Alive* by Aurora Levins Morales and Rosario Morales /$9.95

*The Gilda Stories,* A Novel by Jewelle Gomez/$9.95

*Good Enough To Eat,* A Novel by Lesléa Newman/$8.95

*Humid Pitch,* Narrative Poetry by Cheryl Clarke/$8.95

*Jewish Women's Call For Peace* edited by Rita Falbel, Irena Klepfisz, and Donna Nevel/$4.95

*Jonestown & Other Madness,* Poetry by Pat Parker/$7.95

*Just Say Yes,* A Novel by Judith McDaniel/$8.95

*The Land Of Look Behind,* Prose and Poetry by Michelle Cliff/$8.95

*Legal Tender,* A Mystery by Marion Foster/$9.95

*Lesbian (Out)law,* Survival Under the Rule of Law by Ruthann Robson/$9.95

*A Letter To Harvey Milk,* Short Stories by Lesléa Newman/$8.95

*Letting In The Night,* A Novel by Joan Lindau/$8.95

*Living As A Lesbian,* Poetry by Cheryl Clarke/$7.95

*Making It,* A Woman's Guide to Sex in the Age of AIDS by Cindy Patton and Janis Kelly/$4.95

*Metamorphosis, Reflections On Recovery* by Judith McDaniel/$7.95

*Mohawk Trail* by Beth Brant (*Degonwadonti*)/$7.95

*Moll Cutpurse,* A Novel by Ellen Galford/$7.95

*The Monarchs Are Flying,* A Novel by Marion Foster/$8.95

*More Dykes To Watch Out For,* Cartoons by Alison Bechdel/$7.95

*Movement In Black,* Poetry by Pat Parker/$8.95

*My Mama's Dead Squirrel,* Lesbian Essays on Southern Culture by Mab Segrest/$9.95

(continued)

*New, Improved! Dykes To Watch Out For,* Cartoons by Alison Bechdel/$7.95

*The Other Sappho,* A Novel by Ellen Frye/$8.95

*Out In The World,* International Lesbian Organizing by Shelley Anderson/$4.95

*Politics Of The Heart,* A Lesbian Parenting Anthology edited by Sandra Pollack and Jeanne Vaughn/$12.95

*Presenting. . .Sister NoBlues* by Hattie Gossett/$8.95

*Rebellion, Essays 1980-1991* by Minnie Bruce Pratt/$10.95

*A Restricted Country* by Joan Nestle/$8.95

*Running Fiercely Toward A High Thin Sound,* A Novel by Judith Katz/$9.95

*Sacred Space* by Geraldine Hatch Hanon/$9.95

*Sanctuary, A Journey* by Judith McDaniel/$7.95

*Sans Souci,* And Other Stories by Dionne Brand/$8.95

*Scuttlebutt,* A Novel by Jana Williams/$8.95

*Shoulders,* A Novel by Georgia Cotrell/$8.95

*Simple Songs,* Stories by Vickie Sears/$8.95

*Speaking Dreams,* Science Fiction by Severna Park/$9.95

*Talking Indian,* Reflections on Survival and Writing by Anna Lee Walters/$10.95

*Tender Warriors,* A Novel by Rachel Guido deVries/$8.95

*This Is About Incest* by Margaret Randall/$8.95

*The Threshing Floor,* Short Stories by Barbara Burford/$7.95

*Trash,* Stories by Dorothy Allison/$8.95

*We Say We Love Each Other,* Poetry by Minnie Bruce Pratt/$8.95

*The Women Who Hate Me,* Poetry by Dorothy Allison/$8.95

*Words To The Wise,* A Writer's Guide to Feminist and Lesbian Periodicals & Publishers by Andrea Fleck Clardy/$4.95

*The Worry Girl,* Stories from a Childhood by Andrea Freud Loewenstein/$8.95

*Yours In Struggle,* Three Feminist Perspectives on Anti-Semitism and Racism by Elly Bulkin, Minnie Bruce Pratt, and Barbara Smith/$8.95

**You can buy Firebrand titles at your bookstore, or order them directly from the publisher (141 The Commons, Ithaca, New York 14850, 607-272-0000).**

**Please include $2.00 shipping for the first book and $.50 for each additional book.**

**A free catalog is available on request.**